For all the kids who sent me e-mails, phoned my house and asked for it again and again and again.

Here is your second book.

The Adventures of Dakotaroo
by Krista Michelle Breen

Book One
Quicksand
The Mysterious Disappearance of Dakotaroo

Book Two
Hardware
The Trouble With Phillip

Hardware

The Trouble With Phillip

For Taylor & Dan ♡ horses!

Story and Illustrations by
Krista Michelle Breen

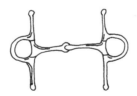

Groundskeeper's Cottage Press

National Library of Canada Cataloguing in Publication Data

Breen, Krista Michelle, 1967 -
          Hardware— The Trouble With Phillip

ISBN: 0-973524-1-1

Groundskeeper's Cottage Press
Box 518
Rockwood, Ontario
Canada N0B 2K0

www.dakotaroo.com

Printed and Bound in Canada

Contents

"I suppose anyone can fall," said Shasta.

"I mean can you fall and get up again without crying and mount again and fall again and yet not be afraid of falling?"

"I-I'll try," said Shasta.

The Horse and His Boy, C.S. Lewis

ONE

Robbie

T.J.'s fingers were just about frozen. She held the clip to undo Dakotaroo's paddock gate in the warmth of her hand to melt the ice. Impatiently the horses leaned forward, their breath becoming streams of warm air, like dragon's smoke. *We want in, we want in now!*

"Quit pushin'," scolded Phillip Brooks, "T.J., why the heck are you just standing there? It's pretty stinkin' cold out here just to be waitin' around for you to open the dumb gate. What's your problem?"

"It's frozen," she replied patiently.

"It's frozen! I'm gonna be frozen in a minute here Teej! Hey," said Phillip looking down at her hand. "Is that the ring your imaginary horse-stealing boyfriend gave you?"

"Yep, I guess so." T.J. was getting pretty tired of Phillip Brooks' endless attempts at teasing her about the disappearance of her horse, Dakotaroo, the previous fall. Phillip, who had just turned 12, spent a great deal of his time thinking of ways to torment people. T.J. was no exception. Every time she turned around it seemed he was moving Dakota into another paddock, hiding her in the storage shed or tying her up in the hay barn. At first the pranks had scared her, now they were just annoying.

Hunching down into her winter coat until her nose touched the cold metal of the zipper, T.J. secretly smiled as she replaced her right glove on her hand. The gate swung open and Dakotaroo followed her silently back to the barn behind Phillip and Doodle the lesson horse. Hoofsteps muffled softly in the fresh fallen snow and pillows of cold air chased them into the barn as they hurried inside. Quickly, T.J. spun Dakota around to close the door. If they left it open for too long the water in the barn could freeze.

Winter on a horse farm in Canada has a strange set of rituals. Thawing frozen things, smashing through icy things, trudging through snowy things. *Tomorrow, you get to do it all again.*

It was then, as they walked the horses through the barn, that T.J. noticed Robbie for the first time. In the middle of what looked like a nest made of an entire square bale of hay, sat a giant gray and brown male goat.

"Like my goat?" asked Phillip. "His name's Robbie. Got him from Ms. Petty yesterday. She said she's gonna be movin' down to Palm Springs, sick of the winter and all, y'know. So she gave me her goat."

Laura Petty ran a large Hunter-Jumper Stable just down the road from Beaverbrook farm. The riders she coached were mostly snooty. T.J.'s best friend Adrienne Brooks made a point of disliking them all.

T.J. looked surprised, "What's going to happen to all her boarders? Where are all those horses going to go?".

"Not here, that's for sure!" Adrienne called out loudly from the feed room. "I'm not havin' any of those wimpy- 'I'm not allowed to take my $40,000 show horse on a hack'- people around here. No way! You gotta have guts to be part of *my* barn." Adrienne held a muffin in her right hand and prepared to continue the tirade.

"Mom's already told some people they can move in." Phillip informed her.

"Great, and *you* have a smelly new friend." Adrienne mocked Phillip while pushing the enormous goat away from her food. "I hate Laura Petty even more now that she isn't around." Adrienne spent most of the winter dressed like an alien. She wore a puffy silver snowmobile suit, with big yellow reflectors, that her Dad had inherited from some old dead uncle. It was extremely ugly, but had about a hundred pockets and was exceptionally warm. Her bushy red hair stuck out crazily from beneath an old fur lined hunter's hat. It was almost hard to tell where Adrienne's hair had stopped and where the hat began.

She took a bite of her muffin as if it was an apple, picked up a scoop of feed in her left hand, and began to do the evening feed. Robbie the goat rocked back and forth for momentum and then stood up to follow her.

"Phillip that's the fattest goat I've ever seen in my whole life. Is it normal?" asked T.J.

"Um, yeah, pretty much," he said slowly, pausing to wipe his nose on his glove. "Ms. Petty said not to expect him to live for too long 'cause he's so overweight. I'm gonna put him on a diet, but if he does die, she asked me to bury him beside that big grave she has for her old Jack Russell."

"I'd get to work on digging a hole right away. Mom's gonna kill both of you if he keeps messing up the hay."

"Maybe you could build him a little cart," quipped T.J. "That'll look real cool."

"Yeah! Hey look everybody, there's Phillip Brooks exercising his freakishly gigantic pet goat!" added Adrienne.

"You're just jealous," said Phillip angrily. "You're all jealous that I got a new goat and you got nothing. Someday Adrienne," Phillip narrowed his eyes into slits, "everyone's gonna be jealous of Robbie."

Within 3 weeks, Laura Petty was gone. Where there used to be horses and people and crazy little Jack Russell dogs, there was now nothing. Quiet. A ghost farm. It gave T.J. the creeps when she rode past it on her bike. A few of Laura's customers had brought their horses up the road to the farm at Beaverbrook Hall. Mostly they were little kids with small ponies, the strange exception being one 18-year-old, long-time student of Laura Petty's by the name of Edward James Dillon III, and his dark bay Hanoverian gelding, Meccano.

Winter was just about to enter a thaw when "Tad" Dillon walked into T.J. and Adrienne's life. Interestingly, it was T.J. who met him first. It was a sunny Sunday afternoon, and the last of the ice on the barn roof was melting and dripping from the tops of the doorways. Adrienne was away from home visiting her grandparents.

T.J. was just finishing grooming Dakotaroo in the cross-ties when a tall young man with dark blonde hair, carrying a saddle, slid through the barn door. She watched quietly for a moment as he began to open the tack lockers one by one.

"C-an I help you?" she asked finally.

"Sure, I'm Tad Dillon," he said, "I need a locker for my stuff. Can I empty one of these?" he said, squinting. The tack lockers were filled with other people's horse stuff. Saddles, bridles, brushes, most of the doors had been decorated with photos and drawings and little pieces of note paper. Tad kept opening the doors looking for an empty one.

T.J. smiled, "There's one way up there," she pointed to a locker on the top row, "It's high up, the little kids don't like it 'cause it's too hard to reach. Actually the only ones around here tall enough to reach those lockers will be you and Adrienne…"

Tad put his saddle in the locker. "Who's Adrienne?" he asked politely, but looked strangely disinterested in what T.J. had to say.

"Adrienne Brooks," she said, surprised by the question. "She lives here. You don't know Adrienne?"

"No."

"Oh, you'll know her when you see her," T.J. nodded and laughed, "She's 15, wears crazy looking riding clothes, sometimes forgets to brush her hair, rides like a maniac all the time," she smiled. "It's pretty hard to miss Adrienne."

"Great, thanks," he said dryly, "…and you are?"

T.J. blushed, embarrassed that she had not introduced herself. "I'm Theresa Jane Thompson," she said cheerfully, "but, everyone calls me T.J. I own Dakotaroo."

The next day, T.J. was helping a little student untack Spanky the lesson pony, when Robbie walked by her and began searching in the young student's tack box for food.

"Ahhhh, help!" yelled the small girl as she tried to pull Robbie away from her precious pail of horse treats.

Robbie's head emerged from the pail holding a clear plastic bag of neatly cut up apple slices. The girl maintained a futile grip on his collar and was being dragged down the hall as T.J. rushed to rescue her.

"You give those back," T.J. scolded, reaching for the goat's collar.

Robbie knew he was no match for T.J. Something had to be done with the apple bag. Something fast. Robbie looked wide eyed at the two girls and just as T.J. reached around to wrestle the bag from his mouth, he stretched his neck forward, moved his pointy tongue around in his mouth, bleated painfully and swallowed hard. The shiny plastic bag and it's priceless treasure of apples disappeared magically into Robbie's mighty mailbox mouth. It was not the first time T.J. had watched an entire plastic bag disappear into Robbie's mouth. It was the first time she had seen him inhale a whole bag of food.

"It's gone?" cried the little girl. "He can eat plastic stuff?" she asked amazed.

"Um, I guess so," said T.J. slowly, still secretly unsure if Robbie was about to drop dead. "Let's go see if there are any carrots in the feed room for Spanky, O.K?" They quietly backed away from Robbie as he reared up on his hind legs. "Remind me again why we needed a goat around here?" T.J. hollered at Adrienne from the other side of the barn.

"Phillip's not right in the head, T.J., just be happy you don't actually have to live with him." Adrienne answered back.

"Oh, trust me, I'm pretty happy Phillip and I don't share any of the same DNA too!" she laughed. "Hey Adrienne, did you get a chance to meet that Tad guy yet?"

"Todd?"

"Tad."

"Ted?"

"No Tad." T.J. said laughing, "He's really quite nice."

"Tad? What kinda name is Tad? Like a baby frog, like a tadpole?"

"Maybe. I don't know what it's short for. That's just his name. Anyhow he's a good rider, I think you'll like him."

Adrienne looked at T.J. seriously. "How do you come to *my* place to ride your horse, the place in the world, might I add, that you are the least likely to find a male human being, and just happen to meet someone?"

T.J. was quiet for a moment, "I'm just fantastically interesting I guess. Please don't bug me about it. I can't help it."

"Oh sor-ry! Yeah, and I'm fantastically intelligent, we're like some super mutant riders. Please don't tease us about our mutant powers." Adrienne said loudly, grabbing her head in her hands and pretending to look anguished.

She unknowingly had an audience.

Tad Dillon had entered the barn through the side door. He stood in the open entrance to the tack room and leaned against the doorstop with his arms folded in front of him. He had perfect teeth.

"Is she going to be O.K.?" he asked T.J..

"Yes," T.J. laughed.

14

"That 'fantastic super intelligence' may come in handy some day," he added smiling.

Adrienne blushed and began to fiddle with her bridle.

"Meccano is in the paddock with the run in shed," said T.J. quickly. "I'm supposed to be working today, so if you need a hand let me know."

"Thanks," said Tad, and choosing a lead from the wall left the barn to bring in his horse.

"If you need a hand let me know." Adrienne mocked T.J. quietly.

"Hey, I could give you some lessons in being nice if you want. Are you going to stay a while and watch him ride?"

"Yeah. O.K." Adrienne paused for a moment and then began to walk in the direction of the indoor arena viewing room. "You'll need to come now though Teej."

"What if Tad needs my help?" asked T.J..

"He won't."

Adrienne entered the dark viewing room, turned on the heater and sat down on the couch. T.J. followed her in.

"Do we get to have some lights on in here?" asked T.J. confused.

"No," whispered Adrienne "and shut up and be quiet. You can see into the arena just fine without the lights on."

T.J. looked at Adrienne in the dark. "This is stupid. Did we come to watch him ride, or to spy on him?"

HARDWARE

"Quiet."

Soon the girls could hear Meccano's hooves walking up the concrete aisle toward the arena. Tad was talking to him.

"Now," said Adrienne "we go here," she stood up and scrambled behind the couch, crouching down. "but we must be totally silent."

"I can't believe I'm doing this." T.J. groaned.

Tad let himself into the arena and prepared to get on. He was tall and thin and wore tight fitting blue jeans under his brown suede half-chaps. His hair was sandy brown, and although long on the top, was cut short at the back and sides so as not to stick out from underneath his riding helmet. His parents divided their time between working in Bermuda and vacationing at their home in the Caledon Hills. At 18, they now trusted Tad to stay in Ontario for long stretches of time without them. Everything about Tad smelled expensive.

Meccano stood about 16.3 hands high at the withers. He was a gorgeous seal coloured dark bay with four white socks. Everything about Meccano was expensive.

"I love that seal colour." T.J. whispered. "I have *always* loved that seal colour."

"And Appaloosas and Greys…," teased Adrienne. " Besides, his coat is only that colour because he has just recently been clipped. Come summer he'll look no different than Annie."

Tad mounted silently and walked him around the arena on a loose rein. After about 5 minutes he picked up a trot.

"Now," said Adrienne, "the moment of truth. Does he really know how to ride his very expensive horse, or is he just another spoiled loser."

"You have a bad attitude." said T.J..

Meccano floated around the Arena. He had style, he had power, and he was attentive to everything Tad asked.

"I don't think that horse looks sound," hissed Adrienne. "Does he look lame to you?"

"Oh Adrienne, give it up. The horse looks awesome. Can we stop spying on him now?"

Just as T.J. stopped talking, Phillip burst through the door and turned on the light. Robbie the goat was right behind him. The commotion of boy and goat and hushes of the girls, quickly caused Meccano to shy away from their end of the arena. Tad looked over in an instant and caught T.J. and Adrienne crouching behind the furniture. He stopped, smiled and shook his head before riding away.

"Phillip!" they both yelled.

"What are you two doing? Are you spying on that guy? What jerks you both are! He's gonna think you're such losers."

Adrienne regained her composure. "Just checking out his horse."

"He's gotta be good, Adrienne. He was in the Canadian Equitation Medal finals last year. That was, of course, 'round about the same time as you two were off playing Cowboys and Indians in *imagination* land."

Robbie lifted his tail, and about a trillion little round goat droppings spilled out of him. The little balls rolled all over the viewing room floor.

"Oooooie, that's so gross!" T.J. laughed.

Robbie turned around and began to smell his manure.

"Hey, you better get your twin brother outta here and clean up that mess before Mom finds out you let him in here."

Phillip grabbed Robbie by the halter and led him towards the door. "Just remember; if he's related to me, he's related to you." Dragging the enormous ruminant along the aisle, he yelled back. "I heard T.J. was working today. Don't let her forget to clean the viewing room."

Adrienne returned to the house and was quickly greeted by her mother.

"Adrienne, did you get a chance to meet Tad, dear?" asked Arleen Brooks as she worked at the computer.

"Yeah, Mom. Nice name." Adrienne replied sarcastically.

"I need you to come here for a minute. I've received an interesting e-mail from Dennison Skyhouse. He has a young horse that he would like to come to us for training this spring." The Skyhouse family bred Appaloosa horses in Palouse River, Montana. Dennison had become friends with the girls when T.J. had loaned his nephew Mickey her horse Dakotaroo for a very important race.

Adrienne rushed over and looked past Arleen's shoulder at the computer screen. "Cool, a horse from *imagination* land," she said. "Can we do it? Please?"

"Slow down a minute. Where's *imagination* land?"

Adrienne laughed, "That's Phillip's annoying way to describe Montana and all the things we did there last fall. Dakotaroo won an *imaginary* race in *imagination* land. Mickey is T.J.'s *imaginary* boyfriend, you get it?"

"Not really. Anyhow, they would like to send us a horse to train to jump. We will have to make sure there's room in the barn, and that you and T.J. will actually do the work." Arleen looked very serious, "You already have a lot on your plate Adrienne. I don't want you to sacrifice your competition schedule just to train horses for Mr. Skyhouse."

"Mom, T.J. is going to be thrilled about this. We can do it. I promise."

"Well, the Skyhouse family were very impressed with Dakotaroo and are convinced that you girls can train another horse to be as brave as her. They are willing to pay a lot of money to have you work their horses. It makes my decision a lot easier, that's for sure."

"Really? Wow! I can't wait to tell T.J. Can I call her right now?"

"You should probably call T.J.'s 'imaginary boyfriend' first," Arleen used Phillip's description for Mickey Skyhouse and smiled,

"The e-mail implied that they would like this to be a surprise for T.J. They wanted to give her a young horse as a gift, but were pretty sure that her family wouldn't appreciate another mouth to feed."

"So she gets a young horse to play with *and* gets paid to work it. That's a pretty good deal, Mom." Adrienne was grinning from ear to ear.

"O.K.. But you girls have to do the work. They won't want to ship their horse 2000 miles for nothing. I'll send a reply to Mr. Skyhouse. You can call Mickey and let him know."

TWO

Torque

Robbie the goat didn't die. He did; however, begin to lose weight no matter how many times he broke into the feed room, ate all of the hot chocolate powder in the lounge, or stole people's lunches. His stomach had taken on an odd football-like shape by mid-April, and he now slept in strange positions just to keep himself comfortable.

T.J. had not received a letter from Mickey Skyhouse in over two months. He never sent messages by e-mail or phoned her. He said he liked old fashioned things. He liked to take his time and write letters that someone would want to keep in a box forever, so that when they died, their friends could open the letters and read all their secrets and cry. T.J. wished he would take the time to write soon.

It was an otherwise normal after school evening, when Mr. Thompson dropped T.J. off at Beaverbrook Hall, with an armful of clean Dakotaroo laundry and a new bag of baby carrots. The afternoon breeze was cold and the ground still mushy from winter, but the sun was shining brightly, as if making a promise to someday warm up the world. T.J. walked the length of the boarder barn, waiting for her eyes to become accustomed to the change in the light, after the brightness of outside.

"He's here!" Adrienne burst through the doorway only minutes after T.J. had arrived.

"Who? Tad?" T.J. asked.

"No silly, come see."

A beautiful, new, 4 horse trailer had pulled into the lane and was parked in the center of the yard alongside the arena. Pulled by a large, white, dual-wheeled pickup truck, the trailer was made of brushed aluminum. It had two individual windows for the horses to look out on either side, and a camper-sleeping area for people at the front. The pickup rumbled. Printed on the side of the trailer, in large turquoise letters, rimmed in tan and white, was one word. Skyhouse.

T.J. stopped breathing. It was as if the trailer had just driven in from out of a dream.

"C'mon." said Adrienne, leading T.J. by the arm to the driver's side of the trailer. "Say hello."

A cigarette came flying out of the driver's window. The door opened, and a well worn cowboy boot stepped out and smashed the cigarette butt into the mud. The emerging driver was short and skinny, his long dark hair held in a single pony-tail.

"Hey there!" he said warmly. "One a'you girls Miss Adrienne

Brooks?"

"Yes." Adrienne smiled, extending her hand in greeting.

T.J. stared at the thin man with her mouth open. He wore a wool lined jean coat and a red and white baseball hat high on his head. His face was very wrinkly and his teeth were badly stained from both coffee and cigarettes. It was difficult to tell how old he was. Thirty, T.J. guessed, maybe older.

"Littlefox," he named himself, shaking T.J.'s hand and giving her a big toothy smile. "Nice place you have here." He hugged his arms around his body for warmth and rubbed his shoulders. "Does it get any warmer?"

The horse in the trailer let out a whinny and was answered by the horses in the barn.

Littlefox nodded in the direction of the trailer. "He's had a long ride, I'm sure Mickey's horse would like to get off the trailer."

It was as though T.J. had not heard him. She just kept watching the truck. "You came alone?" she asked quietly. "All the way from Montana," she sighed, "alone?"

"Oh heck, no!" My cousin Jimmy rode with me until just before the border. He wanted to stop and spend a few days with some old friends so I left him…"

"*Mickey's* horse?" T.J. interrupted.

"Yes!" said Adrienne excitedly. "It's Mickey's new horse. He's here for three months for us to work with over fences. Isn't it cool? Teej, I've been keeping it as a surprise for you for weeks! Man, it was so hard!" she grinned triumphantly.

"*Mickey's* horse?"

Adrienne turned to T.J. and squinted. "Yes. What's wrong with you? Don't you want to see it?"

"Yes."

Littlefox was busy unclamping the catches on the ramp of the trailer and soon disappeared inside. The large gelding backed tentatively off of the trailer, stopping at the bottom of the ramp to smell the air for friends. Littlefox passed the lead to T.J.

"He's a good boy," he said. "Take care of him."

T.J. looked up and rubbed hair above the horse's eyes gently. "Yes, of course." T.J. was still in shock.

"You've had a long drive sir, would you like to come in for a coffee or something? I'm sure my mom would be happy to feed you." Adrienne added.

"Thanks ma'am. But, I gotta go pick up Jimmy before he thinks he needs to get a hotel room for the night. We really have all the things we need in the trailer. It's just like home, thank you kindly." Littlefox walked over to T.J. put his hand on the horse and smiled. "He calls him Torque."

"Thank-you," said T.J., still trying to hide her disappointment.

"Don't you go worry too much, Miss T.J.," he said so only she could hear, "Mickey won't let this horse be outta his sight for too long."

She tried to read the real meaning behind his words. They would echo in her head for a long time. The light of the bright setting sun flashed off the polished aluminum of the trailer, and reflected off the gold of T.J.'s ring as she held Torque by the lead and waved goodbye.

"He's nice, eh?" shouted Adrienne. "This is so cool. We have a horse to train. Someone in the world actually trusts you and me to train their horse to jump. Isn't it awesome?"

"Yeah."

"What? I thought you'd be all excited about this. Mickey sent you a horse all the way from Montana. Look at him!"

"It's great. It's just... I thought...when I saw the trailer..." she paused, "I thought he would visit us too, and then... when that guy stepped out of the truck and he was so wrinkly and old, I just..."

Adrienne looked at T.J. as though she had suddenly become an alien, "T.J. you didn't get a visit from Mickey, but you did get a HORSE!" She waved her arms back and forth in the direction of Torque. "Visit no, horse yes! Visit no, horse yes!" She paused and looked very serious. "T.J., I only want to have to tell you this once, a horse is *always* better than a visit."

"I guess so."

"You guess so!" she laughed. "I know so! Come bring him into the barn so we can take his blankie off and get a good look at him."

It was like unwrapping a present. Under the blanket was the most exquisite horse T.J. had ever seen. His black and white spotted body tapered to a steel grey and ended in long, jet black legs. His mane was black, his tail silver. What T.J. couldn't see, still covered by his tall shipping boots, was that he had four white socks all ending above his knees and hocks.

Adrienne opened the velcro enclosures on the first shipping boot with a zip and let out a slow whistle. "Whew, black legs with white socks! That looks so cool!"

Torque stood quietly in the cross ties and let out a long sigh. His dark eyes were rimmed with white and looked at T.J. like people eyes.

"I think he wants to rest for awhile," said T.J. "That's a really long trailer ride."

"Yeah, he can have the last stall on the left. Leave his blanket off so he can have a good roll if he wants." Adrienne added, standing far back to get a good look at her student. "Pretty funky looking horse, eh Teej? Even I'd have a dumb Appy if I could find one that cool."

"I know where you can get 'em," T.J. smiled.

THREE

The Hermit's Treasure

"Hey there Phil, you taking the Pez pony out on a hack?" Tad asked. It seemed like an odd question to Phillip. All he ever did with Pez was hack, and no one ever really called him "Phil". It sounded weird.

"Yup." Phillip vigorously rubbed Pez between the front legs with a rubber curry comb. Big, fluffy tufts of Pez hair floated to the ground and flew up Tad's nose.

"Do you ever go by the *Massey* farm?" Tad asked slowly.

"I go everywhere." Phillip replied cheerfully, "I actually knew the *Massey* guy. He was pretty cool."

"I read in the newspaper that they're going to auction off all that old guy's stuff next Saturday and I was thinking," Tad smiled, "wouldn't it be kinda cool to go take a look around the place before they do? I kinda like old creepy houses, I'd just like to make a little visit and see how the old dude really lived, y'know?"

"Sure, I guess. Get your horse ready and I'll go with you." Phillip would never admit it, but he did get a little bit lonely exploring places with Pez all the time. Tad's company could be entertaining, and at the very least, Phillip knew that his being friendly with Tad would make Adrienne really, really mad.

The horse's hoofbeats made a wonderful sound on the road, that seemed to ring through the valley. Soon, Phillip turned Pez up the laneway to Bert Massey's. The hedges seemed even more overgrown than he had remembered them. A wind-tattered curtain blew aimlessly out of an open upstairs window. Cats peered at them from inside as they rode past the house.

"Have you ever gone inside?" Tad asked as a challenge.

"Not since the old guy died. I generally go where I'm invited."

Tad looked up to the second story and squinted. "I'm going in. You comin', or are you gonna stay here with the horses."

Phillip did not want Tad to think he was a wimp. Besides, the house looked cold and sad, but not really creepy. Bert had been a little stale smelling and odd, but he was never, ever scary.

"O.K., you can put Meccano in the barn if you want," he told Tad.

The ceiling in the old bank barn was really very low for Meccano's head, and he protested mildly before entering the cold smelly darkness. Two old workhorse standing stalls were in the far end of the barn. Ancient whitewash peeled from the beams and flaked off like snow as the tips of Meccano's ears brushed along them. In most places, the floor was a thick bed of old, dry straw, packed hard and mixed with the manure of some long-gone ruminant. In other spots, the concrete had heaved up with the winter frost and broken violently apart.

"Careful here," said Phillip, "the floor is really uneven." *Robbie would really love it here,* Phillip thought to himself and smiled.

The horses picked their way carefully through the mini boulders of concrete and into the straw of the standing stalls. At the front of the stalls were short, rusty chains. Tad clipped a chain to Meccano's bit and walked away.

"You should probably clip that to your noseband instead." Phillip was surprised that Tad didn't seem to know that what he had done was not very safe. If his horse got frightened when they were away and pulled back from the chain, he could easily injure his mouth.

"Don't tell me what to do, Goat-Boy," Tad said sharply.

They walked across the gravel of the farmyard as Bert must have done a million times in his life. Phillip imagined the old brick house alive with laughter, and warm and cozy inside.

"I bet this was a really nice place once."

"Once," replied Tad. "It's pretty awful now. Do we just walk up and try the door, or do I need to put you through a window?"

"I don't know, Tad. This is kinda like breaking in, especially if I have to go through a window." Phillip was beginning to have second thoughts about looking through old Bert's stuff.

"Chicken."

"No, I just..."

"O.K. chicken, you're probably more use to me as a lookout anyhow. Go around to the front of the house. Stay behind the hedges and bark like a dog if you see anyone walking on the road or driving up the lane. You understand? I'll be listening for a big angry dog, and don't you be taking off to check the horses. I may take a while. Stay at the front of the house."

Tad opened the wooden screen door at the back of the house with a *creak*.

"Shoot," he said trying the brass doorknob, "It's locked. Where d'ya figure the old dude kept his secret key, Goat Boy?"

"He was a hermit, Tad. He never went anywhere. Why would he need a secret key?"

Tad turned the knob on the old door, and slammed hard enough into it to break the hardware and smash the door apart. "Like *my* secret key?" he said with an evil smile as he disappeared inside. "Remember," he yelled back, "woof, woof, woof."

Phillip was quite relieved at being assigned watch duty. A scrawny cat, with one gooey eye stuck shut, followed him behind the hedge.

"Hey buddy," Phillip said to the cat, "that's a pretty gross eye you got there, I wish I had something yummy for you." He decided to call his new friend Mr. Cyclops. Mr. Cyclops the cat.

More than twenty minutes later, Tad emerged from the back door dragging a large green trunk, like a treasure chest but made for a war. It was about the size of a hay bale and appeared to be extremely heavy.

"I could use a hand here," he called to Phillip across the yard.

"What's that?" Phillip asked as he jogged up to Tad. Mr. Cyclops followed cheerfully and was joined by two other equally scrawny young cats.

"A hermit's treasure I believe. It weighs a ton and I can't get it open. Help me drag it to the barn and I'll look for a sledge hammer to bust it up with."

"I don't know, Tad."

"You don't know what? Don'cha want to see what was so important to this weird old dude, that he kept it locked up in here for all these years. Maybe it's the skeleton of his old, dead wife."

"Sure Tad, but I don't think that would be worth getting arrested for."

"Remind me not to bring you along again next time Phillip. Pick up that end of the trunk, if you can."

Phillip was not sure if he *could* lift his side of the trunk. Using

31

both arms on the handle, he managed to get the bottom about an inch from the ground at his end and shuffled across the yard behind Tad. His arms were just about to break off when Tad told him to set it down. The horses, hearing people at the barn door, nickered for food.

"It's getting late Tad," said Phillip looking at his watch. "Eliza gets really upset if we have the horses out on the road at dusk. We should be heading back soon, or she'll freak out."

Tad straightened himself out, and standing tall, rubbed the small of his back. "You're right," he quickly agreed. He didn't really want to open the hermit's trunk with Phillip around anyhow. He wanted to see the treasure by himself.

"Help me get it inside the door and we'll hide it here for now." Tad ordered.

They dragged the trunk into the old barn and pushed it up against the wall. Tad found a bunch of old feed bags, and a mess of old tractor parts and farm garbage and piled it high on top of the trunk. You couldn't tell it was there. Whatever it was in Bert Massey's mysterious treasure box, it was now in his barn. Phillip was beginning to worry.

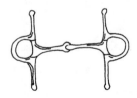

T.J. and Adrienne trotted up behind the boys as they rode along the fourth line heading for home.

A dark blue and silver sedan passed the horses slowly from behind on the road. A man in dark sunglasses in the passenger seat looked at Pez as it passed by.

"Where have you two been?" Adrienne questioned them from on her horse Animation. She was invincible on Animation, she could ask anyone anything and say anything. Tad didn't intimidate her there.

"Massey far..." began Phillip before Tad cut him short.

"Phillip was trying to show me how to get to the Hunt Club the back way, through the Crown Forest. We got lost though and spent a lot of time just smashing through the woods."

Phillip doesn't get lost, thought T.J.

Adrienne looked down at Meccano's clean white polo bandages. "It gets pretty swampy through that way in the spring," she said, squinting at Phillip. "Be careful."

T.J. didn't know what business Tad and Phillip could have had at the Massey Farm. *So you visited the Massey Farm. Who cares*, she thought. It seemed more strange that Tad didn't want them to know.

FOUR

Tad Dillon

There were a lot of things about breaking into Bert's house that really troubled Phillip. The next day at school, all he could think of was how much he didn't want Tad to get his hands on the contents of the green metal box, whatever it was. It was Bert's treasure. An old guy's treasure was not for stealing; an old guy's treasure was for protecting. Some things were *maybe* worth fighting for.

"There's something weird going on, something I can't explain right now, but I really, really need you guys to keep Tad with you this evening."

"And we would want to do this because...?" Adrienne asked cautiously.

"Because I never ask you guys to help me with *anything*, and I think this is really important, and I think he's a creepy jerk."

T.J. squinted, "Perhaps secretly evil?"

"Not secretly, just evil," Phillip replied bluntly.

"Well O.K.," Adrienne sighed. "What do you want us to do."

"I don't know. Maybe take him over to the cross country course at the McLaughlin's or something. *Pretend* you want to show him the jumps. Please."

"Can't," T.J. replied flatly, "The ground's still too mushy. They won't let us on the course yet, and if we sneak on and get caught, we'll be in big trouble."

Phillip bit his bottom lip. "Then ask him to help you with something about your riding. I don't know. Ask him to give you a lesson or something."

"Ne-ver!" Adrienne wailed. "Not in a million years. I'd ask your stupid goat to give me a lesson first."

T.J. could see that this really wasn't getting anywhere. It was true, Phillip never asked for their help with anything, and he had helped T.J. out in the past when she needed it the very most.

"I'll do it." she said.

"What?" said Adrienne.

"I'll do it. I'll ask him to help me with my position over fences or something. I don't mind. Let me go ask him right now before he finishes up with Meccano." T.J. turned Dakotaroo around in the aisle, grabbed her helmet, and set off for the outdoor ring.

HARDWARE

"She's very nice." said Tad as he watched T.J. canter Dakotaroo around the ring. "I'm surprised we never met before. I mean with you keeping her here just up the road from Laura's place and all. Laura would have really liked your horse."

"Oh Laura did like *Dakotaroo*," said T.J.. "She just never really liked me. I don't know why. I met her about 15 times and she was never, ever nice. Adrienne says it's that my parents drive the wrong kind of car."

Tad looked confused, "What difference does it make what kind of car your parents drive?"

T.J. halted Dakotaroo and laughed. "It works like this. If your parents drive you to the barn in an expensive car, Laura knows they have a lot of money to spend, so she treats you nicely. If your parents drive an old junky car, she doesn't bother to notice you. You're not worth her time. If your parents drive an old junky car and you can still

36

beat her students, she starts to treat you *really* badly."

Tad smiled with his perfect teeth, "I think you've put *way* too much thought into this. Maybe you should spend your time talking your parents into buying a nice enough car to match your awesome horse."

"I think Dakotaroo has more money than my parents." T.J. said awkwardly.

"Hey, I heard about all that. She won some big race down in the States last year eh? That must have been pretty cool."

"Yeah, it was cool. I'm just glad she lived through it. The money she won doesn't mean that much really." T.J. turned the ring on her finger, leaned down and gave Dakota a pat. " I'd like to jump a bit today. Could you maybe give me some pointers on my position, or are you in a hurry?"

"Sure thing! Position work is actually my specialty." Tad replied arrogantly. "I can do it this time, but I'm afraid the next time you need some help, I'll have to charge you for my time, O.K?"

He expected to be paid for helping her. The comment was so unexpected, that T.J. had trouble not laughing out loud. Adrienne would have had a fit if she had heard. Laura Petty had apparently taught him well.

"Um, O.K.," said T.J. "Where shall we begin?"

Adrienne watched from out of sight in the barn. Tad instructed T.J. to canter around in 2-point and really concentrate on her leg

37

position. *Baby stuff,* she thought, *man, what a boring position fixer he is*. Now and then the wind would carry Tad's voice toward the barn and Adrienne would cringe at his instructions.

"Arch your back and stick your bum out." Tad hollered. "Smile, smile more T.J., the judge wants to see you smile."

Poor T.J., thought Adrienne. *Phillip's gonna owe her big time for this.*

They worked Dakotaroo for a good 45 minutes before returning to the barn. With her back to Tad, T.J. rolled her eyes and led Dakota past Adrienne. Adrienne swept the barn and smiled.

"Wow Adrienne," Tad said, "Teej just had an awesome lesson with me. You really should have come down to watch. She's got a great little horse there. It's just that her whole way of riding is so 'back-yard', y'know. Not to say anything against Eliza, she's a fine riding teacher for beginners. I just think you guys could stand to bring things up a notch around here."

"You think so, eh?" Adrienne sounded only a little bit sarcastic. If you didn't know her well you probably wouldn't detect it.

"I know so," he replied. "I've been to all the big 'A' Circuit hunter shows. I know what it takes to win."

"Good for you," Adrienne smiled and nodded. This time she really did sound sarcastic. "Too bad there aren't any hunter classes at the Olympics eh? It's just so thrilling."

"Adrienne, what's your problem?" Tad turned and asked unexpectedly.

"Pardon me?" she snapped back.

"You walk around like we're all supposed to worship you. I, in case you haven't figured it out, am a customer of your mother's. Meccano and I pay the bills. *You* could work a little harder at making the customers feel welcome. Especially the new ones. I'm just trying to help around here."

Adrienne squinted back at him, "I just don't think my mother should take in Hunter riders as boarders. I mean it's not really what we're into. I'd rather watch paint dry than ever watch another dumb Hunter show and you're here telling me that T.J. and Dakotaroo, who could kick your tail in a roll back turn, are back-yardy? We like the back yard, thanks. That's where the good riders are."

"*Maybe* you just don't understand the discipline."

"*Maybe* I think you're a crappy rider."

Tad narrowed his eyes and coldly ran his hand along Meccano's smooth, shining coat. He took a deep breath and feigned a sigh, "Well, truth is, Adrienne," he paused, "everyone thinks *you're* a crappy rider with a nice expensive horse. That's what they all say about you, Adrienne, like it or not." Slowly he turned, kicked over the cat food and left the barn. His words would have more of an impact on Adrienne than he ever would have expected.

FIVE

Phillip The Pirate

It was still there. Phillip dismounted Pez and walked over to where Tad had covered the large metal trunk with junk in the old barn. It was still there. He could see a cold green corner peering out at him from one end.

Outside, Robbie stood on his hind legs and ate the first few leaves off of a small poplar tree.

"Hey goat, don't you get us in trouble here," Phillip warned quietly, quickly looking around before uncovering the trunk and trying for the first time to open it on his own. It was no use. Someone had designed this trunk, long ago, to keep people out. It's secrets were still safely inside.

"We have to hide this from Tad," he told Pez. " It's really stinkin' heavy so we gotta think of a way to move it ourselves; you, me and the goat."

Robbie was beginning to wreak havoc in the overgrown flowerbeds around the house. His large round body and indiscriminate love of vegetation, had quickly transformed the gardens from overgrown and abandoned, to trampled and tasted. He had to be stopped.

"Robbie!" scolded Phillip. "Come here."

Robbie did not come.

"Oh, man," said Phillip, leaving Pez to stand alone and rushing over to extract Robbie from the lilacs. "You will have to wait in the barn until I can figure this out." He dragged the ambling goat along by the collar to the door of the barn. Pez was more than happy to explore someone else's barn for food. Phillip tied Robbie to an old rope wrapped around a post. Pez scattered the dusty straw on the floor with the breath from his nostrils.

"Blaaa," Robbie protested. "Blaaa."

"Shhh…Stay quiet so I can think." Phillip sat down on the old concrete cattle feeder. Maybe if he could find a rope or something Pez could pull the trunk someplace else. Someplace safe from Tad. *What the heck would Bert have done?* Phillip leaned back and surveyed the whitewashed stone walls of the inside of the barn. Barn swallows peeked out at him suspiciously from inside their little mud nests. Finally, far in a corner and partially covered by some giant old burlap bags, he found an answer.

Two old sets of heavy work horse harness were hung high in the rafters. The thick leather was dry, but double stitched and still strong.

The bit and all the fittings were made of some brassy metal that had gone green and crusty. The harness just might do.

Pez did not look very impressed as Phillip climbed a rickety stack of crates to heave the harness from the wall.

"Look Pezzer man!" he said, letting the giant tangle of leather and metal crash to the floor. "Let's figure this baby out!"

Pez had been trained to drive and knew how to wear a light harness well. This was not light harness.

"Mmm..." said Phillip excitedly, "I think it needs some kind of collar or something." He squinted. "Collar, collar, collar, collar, collar...," he said looking through the other old dusty stuff on the walls. There was no collar. "Collar, collar, collar, collar, collar..." He left the animals and climbed the broken old whitewashed stairs up to the hay loft of the barn.

"Blaaaa," protested Robbie as he left.

"Collar!" Phillip came back down the stairs with a flat old, worn out horse collar. He plopped it over Pez's head and smiled. "Beautiful Pezzy, you look awesome."

Pez stared back at him.

"Now how the heck does the rest of this work?" Phillip spent the next half hour spreading the various harness parts out on the floor of the barn. There were indeed, two unique sets. The bridle for the horse's head, the heavy metal hames to attach the harness to the collar, and the long leather traces that lead from the collar to the thing that needed to be pulled, were easily identified. Everything else was a bit of a mystery.

"I guess we can just go with what we know," he said to the pony. "I think we could use your regular bridle instead of this crusty old green thing. Then I could just ride like normal while you pull the trunk." He smiled and began attaching the hames to the collar and the traces to the hames. Bridle, saddle, collar, traces, Phillip pulled down his stirrups and ran the traces through them to the back of Pez. It just looked like a good idea. "Close enough," he said, "come."

The trunk had handles, and was easy to attach the pony to. Pez leaned into the collar and happily pulled the treasure along. Phillip knew one place in the forest that he had never shown to Tad. A secret, forgotten place where he went to be alone, that not even T.J. and Adrienne had ever found. Pez knew the way.

He had found the place, completely by accident, only days after Bert had died. It had frightened him at first, sitting quietly by itself in the dappled sunlight of the forest. A tiny old wooden house, alone, abandoned in the trees. A hideout where a real hermit could live. It gave Phillip the creeps.

The day he found it, he sat for awhile on Pez, a distance away, trying to decide if anyone did live in the shack.

"Hello?" he said sheepishly, "Hello there? Anyone home?"

43

HARDWARE

The roof was covered in moss. The glass had, for the most part, been smashed out of the windows, and the bricks of the chimney had begun to flake and crumble away. The longer he sat with deer flies sticking to Pez's ears, the more he watched and noticed how the spider webs had grown over the corners of things, the more the little house seemed to present itself as an opportunity rather than a threat. A secret opportunity; a secret home. Phillip rode Pez up to the front door, slid off silently, and took a peek inside.

It was open, not enough to squeeze through, just a crack. Phillip pushed the handle and opened the door slowly. It was wonderful. It smelled of dirt, and wood, and worms, and mould. On the walls were long shelves and old posters of tractors, and there was a large old table in the center of the room with an odd assortment of unmatched kitchen chairs. The chimney above led down to a large metal monster. *Like a stove and a bathtub welded together,* thought Phillip. *Sugar bush*, he suddenly remembered. Bert called the forest, *the sugar bush*. For a hundred years Bert's family had used this forest to make maple syrup. Phillip looked at Pez and gave him a smile. He had found the secret Sugar Shack. No other kid he knew had a real shack of their own. Phillip Brook's amazing collection of unwanted junk and cool contraptions had finally found a home.

In the spring, when the sun warmed the tops of the trees and the sap from the maples started to flow, he invited his father out with him to the bush and showed him the shack. Mr. Brooks got them permission from Bert's estate, and together they had tapped the trees and made 60 jars of pure maple syrup on secret trips to the sugar bush after school. Phillip collected up the pails from the trees, his dad lit the fire in the fire box, and together they talked and ate junk food while the water evaporated from the light golden syrup. They laughed a lot about how it was what old Bert would have wanted them to do.

Surprisingly, Phillip found that you could drag the mysterious green trunk by it's handles through the bush for miles, and inflict very little damage on it. It was already scratched and old looking, but dragging it didn't wreck it at all. It flipped over, bounced along, skidded through boulders, squashed through trees and still refused to smash open. The further they rode through the woods, the more amazed Phillip became. Nothing was going to destroy this big metal box. He thought about rolling it down a cliff, or throwing a rope over a tree branch and getting Pez to haul the trunk high into a tree so they could drop it from up high. "We can't do it," he said cheerfully to Pez and thinking out loud, "If we want to see this treasure without smashing it to bits we *need* to find a way to break the lock," he paused, "or find Bert's secret key."

Torque had been trained in a strange western way, that seemed to T.J. to involve always going super, extra slowly. He could have cantered on a skateboard. T.J. found it fairly annoying. Why walk with energetic, large strides when you could just trot painfully slowly? Why trot like a normal horse when you could canter teeny, tiny strides? Before he could be taught to jump, he needed to learn to put more effort into his work.

"It's funny," she said to Eliza, "He's a lovely big horse with a teeny-tiny slow motion canter. It's cool for about 2 seconds, or maybe for old folks. It's not really a canter you can jump a horse from."

"Hack him," said Eliza, "Take him out on the road and through the trails with an older horse. Let him have a little fun and learn that you're not going to get angry when he moves strong."

So they set up a schedule: two days a week T.J. worked on Torque's jumping; two days a week T.J. or Adrienne were to hack him with either Dakotaroo or Annie; once a week Eliza worked on his Dressage. Mickey's horse had become quite a team effort. They all wanted to show Dennison Skyhouse that if he gave them nice horses, they would come home to him as great horses. The only way to do it was through hard work. No horse ever got to be great just standing around in the paddock all day.

Phillip was walking between the stables and the house, when Tad's silver Honda slowly pulled up beside him.

"Goin' home?" asked Tad.

"Um, yes, the house is right there," he pointed, "Where else would I be going?"

"Hop in," Tad said, "I'll give you a lift."

"To the house? It's O.K. I'll walk."

"I went by the Massey place today." Tad said coldly. "Hop in."

Phillip's heart began to race. *Stay calm*, he thought, *act normal, do as he says and everything will be fine.* "So you went by the Massey place, you go treasure hunting again?"

"The trunk is gone."

"Real-ly, wow, that's odd." Phillip sat on his hands to stop them from shaking.

"No." Tad pulled the car beside the garage at the house and looked at himself in the rearview mirror before he slowly turned to look at Phillip. "I was there when he died you know."

It was the first thing that Tad ever said that truly frightened Phillip. Phillip was hoping that he was lying and stayed quiet.

"What? You don't believe me. I was there. In the kitchen. Laura

47

took me." He leaned in close and dropped his voice to a whisper as if anyone was around to hear. "They had a fight, I think they had been fighting for years really. It was a strange argument, about T.J.'s horse, and a lion. It was round about the same time as T.J.'s dumb horse got into all that trouble down south. Laura told him she would find the horse, if he gave her the lion."

Phillip looked confused. Dakotaroo had technically been in trouble up north. Tad was apparently a creepy jerk with a poor sense of geography. What did Laura Petty know about the disappearance of Dakotaroo, and when was the part when Bert died? "L- l- l- aura killed him?"

Tad laughed. "No. She was actually really angry the old dude up and died. He did, right then and there, took some weird kind of fit and dropped dead on the floor. Laura was freakin' out. She cursed and swore and yelled at me not to touch him or anything in the house."

"Why are you telling me this? Shouldn't you be talking to the police."

"She didn't *kill* him Phillip. He just died. The police know that, I was her witness."

"How does the trunk fit into all this."

"The Lion. The lion is in the trunk, that's what I figure anyhow. Laura asked that I get her the trunk and put it in a safe place until she got back from the States. The old guy, he died without leaving a will

48

you see. They're gonna auction off all his stuff next Saturday. Laura didn't want the trunk in the auction. She paid me five thousand dollars to make sure it never made it there."

"An old dead dried up lion?" Phillip had trouble imagining what that would look like in a box. A skull, dry old mane hair, pointy teeth, it was kind of gross and he was now quite glad that he had not been able to open the trunk by himself.

"I guess."

"Why are you telling me this?"

"I like you Phillip, I like you as a friend. You remind me of myself as a kid. You don't really care about anyone or anything now do you?"

Phillip stared at Tad angrily with his bright amber eyes but said nothing. He did care, he cared about lots of things. He cared about Bert.

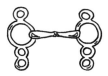

SIX

The Lion of Shalasa

By Saturday morning the entire contents of Bert Massey's house had been removed and spread outside on long tables and hay wagons. It was as if the house had neatly vomited out all of Bert's life for the neighbours to see. Phillip left home on his bike and arrived at the auction early. The grass, still wet from the dew, sparkled brightly in the morning sun. As he parked his bike by a tree, Phillip felt strangely happy and sad at the same time. He had one fifty dollar bill in his pocket. Fifty dollars his grandmother had given him for his birthday. He wanted to buy something cool of Bert's.

Bert had a lot of cool stuff. In his younger days he had traveled the world, fought in the war and worked as an assistant for an archeologist. He had Zebra skin rugs, Antelope heads, giant Nautilus fossils and all kinds of strange African art. Phillip wandered through the collection under the watchful eye of the Auctioneer's wife. Tad it seemed, had slept in and was about to miss out on the fun.

They began the auction with machinery and the contents of Bert's barn. Phillip wandered over to a large clothes rack and began trying on some of Bert's hats, when on the ground he noticed another large trunk. Older than the impermeable metal box he had rescued from Tad, this trunk was metal strapped with wood and looked far more like a pirate's treasure chest.

"It's a steamer trunk," said a strange woman's voice while Phillip looked at it curiously. "In the olden days when people traveled by ship, they put their belongings in steamer trunks. This one is quite lovely."

Phillip ran his hand gingerly along the metal and wood lid of the trunk. When he came to the latch it was unlocked and opened easily.

"Careful son," said the woman.

Phillip lifted the lid and peered inside. The contents smelled musty and warm. The inside of the lid was printed with an old illustration of people looking out to a ship at sea. The inside of the trunk was full of tiny treasures and a box of old photographs.

"How would I be able to buy this trunk?" Phillip quickly asked, looking up at the lady beside him.

"You need a number. You can get one from the auctioneer's table by the front porch," the woman answered politely before pushing past him to look into the trunk.

"Will it be expensive?" he asked.

The woman smiled sweetly at him and laughed, "It's an auction dear," she said, "You never, ever know."

HARDWARE

Bidding on the steamer trunk didn't begin until 2:30. Phillip had a lot of time to look at all Bert's old stuff by then, and had come to the conclusion that unless it was well hidden in an old jar or sewn into the lining of one of Bert's suit jackets, the key he searched for was not there. Phillip still wanted the musty trunk to add to his collection, and had bid and purchased an old felt fedora of Bert's just for practice. For lunch Phillip had bought a wonderful big hot dog from a vendor leaving him exactly $34.95 left in his pocket when the trunk hit the stand. Four people besides Phillip decided they needed the trunk. He stood right at the front of the crowd and raised his number high to let the auctioneer know for sure, that every time the price went up, he indeed wanted to stay in the bidding game.

"Five? Five? Who'll give me five? Lookin' for five. Five. Ten? Ten. Twelve? Twelve. I've got twelve.."

Phillip pulled the large,` grey hat low down over his eyes to make himself look more serious.

"Twenty-five? Twenty-five. Original 1850 steamer trunk here. Thirty. Thirty-five?"

Two of the other bidders dropped out at thirty.

"I've got thirty, lookin' for thirty-five, anybody gonna give me thirty-five?"

Phillip had $34.95. There was nothing else he could do. "Thirty-two!" he yelled. "I'll give you thirty-two!"

"Thirty-two!" hollered the auctioneer, "young man in the hat gonna give me thirty-two. Anybody got thirty-five? Thirty-five? Thirty-five?"

The crowd grew quiet for a moment.

"Thirty-five!" yelled a woman from far in the back.

"Forty?" bellowed the auctioneer and stared hard at Phillip. "Forty?"

He was done. Beat out of the bidding at Thirty-five dollars. The hot dog and the hat had kept him from winning the treasures of the trunk. *Oh well, it is a pretty cool hat.* Phillip sighed and started to walk slowly to the back of the crowd. Lots of old folks were smiling and nodding at him. It was like an approval, like the musty old auction goers were happy to have a young guy at the party. Phillip sheepishly smiled back; until suddenly, a bony old hand reached out and grabbed him at the elbow.

"Would you like something from the trunk son?" said a hoarse woman's voice.

"Pardon me?" replied Phillip.

HARDWARE

"The trunk," she said, "the trunk you bid on son, was there something you wanted from inside the steamer trunk."

The woman had surprised Phillip so much that at first he didn't know what to say.

"Sometimes," she continued, "people will bid on a box full of things just for one item. I only really want the trunk, if there's anything inside it you would like, you are welcome to take it."

Phillip stared at the tiny woman and swallowed hard. "Um, the photos," he said. "I was hoping to get the box of photos."

The woman laughed. "The photos? You were willing to pay $35 just for a box of Bert Massey's photos?"

He dropped his eyes. "Yup, I guess so."

"Hey, don't be embarrassed, we all collect different treasures y'know, if you want that box of photos so bad, you can have it y'hear? I only really want the trunk. All that other stuff is just garbage to me."

Phillip took the precious box of photos back to the sugar shack and began to look through them. There were pictures of Bert in uniform, Bert and some other fellows in the jungle, Bert at the Pyramids. One photo was of Bert and a young, likely yearling, Appaloosa horse. He was wearing a cowboy hat and receiving a giant silver plate from a beautiful girl with long dark hair. Phillip looked at the picture for awhile and then put it aside from the box. It was not half as interesting as Bert at the Pyramids, but he figured the girls might be interested in "Cowboy Bert". There was also quite an assortment of newspaper articles folded among the photos. At first Phillip didn't realize what they were. Although the print and photos remained crystal clear, the newsprint had turned from grey to almost orange. He carefully unfolded them one at a time.

Canadian Man finds The Lion of Shalasa.

SALISBURY, RHODESIA, A young Canadian has unearthed the fabled "Lion of Shalasa" deep in the ruins of a Nubian temple here on the outskirts of Salisbury. Bert Massey, working as a research assistant to famed Egyptologist Dr. Alexander Bromwell, discovered the 54 Carat diamond lodged between two giant rocks forming the last remaining wall of the temple. "Someone went out of their way to hide the diamond here." said Dr. Bromwell, "The Nubians were at war and final days of the temple were filled with violence." The Lion of Shalasa may have remained in hiding for many more years were it not for the keen eye of Massey. "I was just finishing up my measurements and recording the last data of the day when the sun caught the edge of the stone and made a reflection on the sand. It was a bit of a trick to follow the reflection to its source, but in the end, by gum, there she was."

Phillip spent the rest of the afternoon reading news reports about Bert and his famous diamond. It had traveled to museums around the world. Bert had always traveled with it. He didn't want any one particular museum to own it, and since the part of Africa he found it in was frequently at war, he didn't feel it would ever be safe there. It was only safe with him. The Lion of Shalasa, ancient diamond of the Nubians. The Lion of Shalasa was in the trunk. Laura had paid Tad five thousand dollars to keep it out of the auction. He now knew why. Phillip stood up and lifted the old musty piece of carpet he had placed under the table at the center of the room, and with a small camping shovel, he began to dig a hole large enough for the trunk to fit into the floor.

SEVEN

The Sugar Shack

Adrienne was becoming very fond of Torque. It was never very clear to T.J. why. Maybe because Adrienne had heard, just one too many times, how everyone really believed she was just a crappy rider with an expensive horse. Torque looked expensive but everyone knew he was still green and had miles and miles to go in his training. Together T.J. and Adrienne shared the workload in bringing Torque along. They both knew the more times he was ridden, before he had to go home, the better the horse he would be.

Sunday, the day after the auction at the Massey Farm, the Pony Club held a clinic at a farm on the Fourth Line. It was good training for Torque to get out and see some different kinds of jumps, he was well behaved and attracted quite a crowd. Mr. Thompson trailered the girls over in the morning, but the farm was close enough to ride back, so he left them there and went golfing. Most of the way home they could take the rail trail. There was only about a half mile where they needed to cut across some farmers' fields to join back up to the Third Line. Each time they made the trip from the rail trail home, Adrienne would make them try a different path. Sometimes they got desperately lost. Sometimes they were eaten alive by mosquitos, and still other times they ended up riding through the river. For Adrienne it was all about the adventure.

"Have you ever been down that trail?" she asked, pointing her crop to a wide, overgrown, side branch off the main trail.

"No, I never noticed it before, but something went through there recently." said T.J. looking at the ground. "What do you think made that weird kind of track?"

Adrienne had not noticed at first, but the mud on the side trail was smushed in a flat line about the width of a hay bale. "I don't know? Could it have been a snowmobile?"

"Maybe a stolen one, who else but a thief would bring a snowmobile through here in the mud and all. You'd wreck it. The track seems too smooth though, a snowmobile would crunch it up more."

"Golf cart?"

"Not wheelie or wide enough."

"Giant mutant slug?"

"Yes, perhaps," smiled T.J.

"Let's go see what's there," said Adrienne moving Torque in front and starting up the trail. Dakotaroo quickly lurched forward and pushed the big grey horse aside to take the lead. "What's with her?"

"I don't know Adrienne, it must be him. I think she's in love."

"Please, we have enough of that." Adrienne teased.

The trail wound softly through the bush. The trees were a good ten feet apart and a car or truck could have easily negotiated the path.

"This is almost like an old road, I bet it's been here a long time. Look how big the trees are on either side."

"Somebody has been maintaining this trail." Adrienne noted, "No little trees have been allowed to grow up along the pathway at all. Look, the branches of the bigger trees have even been trimmed to keep it neat."

"Who owns this section of bush anyhow Adrienne?"

"Um, probably Bert Massey did." Adrienne said quietly. "The footing is great here? Do you want to canter for awhile."

"Sure." T.J. smiled and asked Dakota to canter.

The horses sprang to life. T.J. bridged her reins, she'd ridden with Adrienne Brooks long enough to know what was coming next.

"Faster!" yelled Adrienne from behind. "Lets see if this beastly boy can catch you yet!"

T.J. moved into galloping position and pushed Dakota forward. The carpet of last years leaves flew beneath her feet as Dakotaroo became part of the wind. Torque powered along behind her, his thick sturdy legs and oversized feet finding easy purchase in the soft sticky mud. They rounded a long slow corner, Torque had moved up on Dakotaroo and was cheekily trying to bite at her haunches. Adrienne hissed and kicked him forward.

"Learn some manners!" she hollered at the big horse and brushing him gently with her crop sent him forward, in front of Dakotaroo. "See you up ahead Teej, I'm gonna see what this baby does without his girlfriend for a while." Adrienne swished her crop again and tucked low down to gallop even faster through the forest. In an instant they were gone from T.J.'s sight around the next bend.

T.J. and Dakotaroo cantered along happily for a while. It was *really* important for Torque to learn to leave his friends and work confidently on his own. He needed to learn to trust his rider more, unfortunately for Adrienne, today was probably not the best day. Rounding their third corner since leaving the security of Dakotaroo's company, Torque found himself confronted with an odd little wooden building sitting right beside the trail. He raised his head as he passed to get a better look. Suddenly, something hit Adrienne in the chest. She flew through the air over the back of the horse and landed hard against an old tree.

It was a few minutes before T.J. noticed Adrienne had come off. At first, when she approached Torque standing quietly beside the small shack T.J. assumed Adrienne had just dismounted to take a look at the building. It was not until Dakota was almost on top of Adrienne that

60

The Sugar Shack

T.J. saw her on the ground. Adrienne sat on her butt with her knees tucked up under her chin and her arms wrapped around her head. Her eyes were closed tight.

"Hey! Are you alright?" T.J. asked with alarm, quickly vaulting from Dakotaroo.

For a while Adrienne was quiet. "Um," she said finally, " I went headfirst into that tree." Her eyes were still closed.

"Seriously?" T.J. squatted down and pulled a muddy twig from Adrienne's lips. " Are you O.K?"

"Yeah," she said slowly, running her tongue around the front of her teeth. She could taste blood and feel the grit of a chipped tooth in her mouth but couldn't figure out why or where exactly it had come from. "Yeah, just give me a minute."

T.J. looked around. They were beside a low old wooden building. It was strange. The little house had a small brick chimney, one door and one old glass window missing most of it's panes. The roof was made of ancient cedar shakes and the whole building was covered in thick green moss, as though it had just grown up out of the forest. "What happened?"

"Look up," she answered. "There's a clothesline across the trail. Torque went under, I got hung up." She swallowed.

Sure enough, a grey plastic coated metal-cable clothesline was strung from tree to tree across the path. Six or seven old wooden

61

clothespins still hung on the line. T.J. shuddered "Adrienne, you're lucky you're not dead." Strangely, although it was not the kind of thing Adrienne really liked to hear, it was not the first time T.J. had ever said those words.

"Yup." Adrienne closed her eyes tight again.

"That's creepy," said T.J. "Adrienne," she said looking all around. " This place gives me the creeps. Can we go or are you really hurt."

"Yup." said Adrienne again. Her ears were ringing.

T.J. was beginning to worry that she was really hurt. "Should I go for help?"

"No. I'm O.K.," Adrienne replied and then paused. "It's just my head, bring Torque over here and I'll ride home." She waved her arm slowly in the direction of the big horse. T.J. could see the blood in her mouth for the first time.

"Are you sure? Here, you can ride Roo."

"No, I'm fine. Been worse. Let's go." Adrienne got up slowly and mounted Torque by herself. The sunlight seemed really bright.

It was not the first time T.J. had endured being the friend of Adrienne crashing. Adrienne did reckless things and sometimes paid the price. She rarely told her parents when she took a bad fall, it was always up to Eliza or T.J. to decide when she had crossed the line between brave and beaten. Riding home, T.J. kept a close eye on her as they cantered back to the Third Line, secretly afraid she would somehow, suddenly, pass out. Adrienne was so quiet she moved like a machine. Someday, T.J. knew, they'd have a big laugh about the day Adrienne hit a clothesline and came flying off, and how T.J. was too chicken to stay by the little shack till Adrienne felt well enough to ride. Today was not going to be that day.

Arleen Brooks sat at the long pine kitchen table. Her expression was serious. Arleen Brooks never sat and was rarely serious. In front of her on the golden table was a glossy 8" x 10" photo of a dark bay horse in lime green polo wraps galloping across a beautiful wide open green field.

"A wedding guest caught you galloping across the golf course last Saturday night. They have pictures," she said sadly. "Adrienne, they're ready to charge you twenty-five dollars for each hoof print on the fairway. When your father gets home from Calgary, the two of you can meet with the course superintendent and figure out how you're going to pay for the damage."

Adrienne went pale. Her head was still ringing from her fall from Torque. She held on to the table for support and leaned over to look at the photo. "Mom, it's not me." she said quietly.

T.J. moved beside her and squinted hard at the picture.

"That's not me!" Adrienne protested louder.

"Adrienne, how am I supposed to believe you? I'm afraid, I'm going to have to ground you from leaving the property with any horse for the remainder of the week."

"It wasn't me mom, I swear!" Adrienne pleaded helplessly.

"Adrienne, a man who has never met you, described your horse perfectly. He knew that you wore a black helmet cover and a lime green vest. He seems confident that the rider he saw was you, and *you* haven't given me a single good reason to believe otherwise."

"You can believe me, because I'm me."

"You did jump Mr. Chacia's rose hedge and park bench as a two stride combination last year. You didn't think anything of tearing up *his* grass now did you?" Arleen fumed.

Adrienne smiled, "Yeah, but that was different. I really needed to be the first one to jump through there. It was brilliant. The distance between the bench and the hedge was just perfect. Too bad we don't have a picture of that, with the roses and everything."

"I liked the old grandma lady chasing us down the road with a broom." T.J. was secretly pleased to see Adrienne was in a fighting mood.

"It's you Adrienne, your horse, your hockey sweater, your polos, your helmet. Why can't you be honest with me? Why do you and your brother always have all these little secret missions going on behind my back?"

Adrienne looked serious. She was rarely serious either. "Mom," she said finally. "If this is Annie, something very secret is going on behind all of our backs."

Before T.J. left Beaverbrook for the evening, and set out to ride her bike home, she took a detour from the house down to the barn. She found Phillip, watering the horses and tormenting the students.

"Hey there," she said quietly.

"Hey."

"Um, could you keep an eye on Adrienne for me tonight. I know it's a lot to ask of you."

Phillip smiled, "Yeah, why, she come off again today?"

"Yeah, she hit her head hard on a tree. She's not going to tell your mom, I know it. Your mom's all mad because someone sent her a picture of Adrienne riding on the golf course."

"Did she?"

"No. I don't know. It's weird. Adrienne say's it's not her but it sure looks like Annie to me. Something funny is going on. Adrienne brags about everything, why would she keep this a secret? Your mom has the picture, get a good look at it and tell me what you think."

"Yeah, no problem." Phillip was quiet for a moment, looked at Robbie munching quietly in the hay and took a deep breath, " T.J." he said, his voice quivering, "There's something I need to tell someone. Something bad is happening and I don't really know if I can fix things alone."

"What's up?"

"Um, well, y'know that old hermit guy Bert that lived up the road."

"Yeah, I didn't know him, but I know of him," she replied honestly.

"Tad was there when he died," he paused. "Tad didn't kill him or anything, the police know he was there. It was an accident or something. It's just that, now he's trying to steal the old guy's treasure."

"Bert Massey had a treasure?"

"Yup." Phillip was reluctant to tell T.J. anything about the Lion of Shalasa or the fight about it and Dakotaroo. He still wasn't a hundred percent confident that it was indeed in the trunk. "My problem is that Tad stole it from Bert's house," he looked straight through her with his bright amber eyes, "and now I've stolen it from Tad."

T.J. was amazed, Phillip really needed someone to confide in right now and he had chosen her. "It's O.K. Phillip," she said, "everything is going to be alright."

Phillip started to cry. "I don't know Teej. You don't understand, this is *really, really* bad. He knows I've got it, I can tell. He's gonna flip if he finds it."

"Hey, easy," she said putting her arm around his shoulders. "where have you got the treasure now? Here, on the farm?"

"No," he looked around and then whispered. "It's in a big green metal trunk from the war. Pez dragged it from Bert's barn to an old sugar shack way back in the bush behind his farm. It's my hideout. I've had it for a while now…"

"A falling down old wood shack with a crumbly brick chimney and a clothesline across the trail?"

"You've been there?"

"Yes, Adrienne found the clothesline with her chest today. Way to go Danger Boy, that's a nice way to get a rider killed."

"Eeeewww, I never thought of that, Pez is short enough to go underneath and I just thought it looked kinda cool. Anyway yes, that's the place. It's there, but I can't open it. It needs some odd old key. I'm trying to find the key before Tad finds the sugar shack."

"Good luck with that. The key could be anywhere." T.J. laughed and then immediately felt badly when Phillip began to get upset again. "Sorry, listen, you have to ask Adrienne to help. Tad's no match for Adrienne and you know it. She can be tougher and meaner than anyone. You *need* to let her help you."

Phillip wiped his drippy nose on his sleeve.

"Truth is, Adrienne actually *likes* helping people. She just pretends she doesn't care about anything so people make a big fuss when she fixes things. Besides, I know for a fact, she can't stand Tad. If you tell her he's pushin' you around, or you need him out of your road, you know she'll be after him in a minute. If you can't find the key, we can always just be like pirates, dig a hole and bury the trunk where Tad'll never find it."

Phillip sniffled, "Yeah Teej, you're right," he sighed with relief and was quiet.

T.J. turned the ring on her finger. "Phillip," she said softly, "could you do me a favour? Like, well, you're good at researching things and stuff and I have something I need to know."

"Sure Teej, anything."

"Well, I have this ring y'know, and well, I'd like to know how Mickey's parents died." she explained sheepishly.

Phillip looked puzzled, "Why don't you just ask him?"

"I don't know. I don't want to ask him, but I need to know. It's just kinda weird wearing a ring that's special, and not knowing anything about the person that used to wear it. Who she was, what she liked, how she died? Does this make any sense to you?"

"I guess, well, all except the part where you don't want to ask Mickey about it yourself." Phillip was slowly becoming Phillip again.

"Will you do it for me though?" T.J. asked.

"Sure Teej," Phillip smiled warmly, "anything for you."

EIGHT

Thief

He could do it all without turning on the lights. First the polos,
lime green on all four and then the boot polish, black to cover any white
bits of the horse left uncovered by the wraps. No saddle, black saddle
pad, black helmet cover, lime green body protector. They walked
quietly out the back door of the barn and through the far side of the
Arena. Silently he mounted, pulled a map from his pocket and quickly
checked it with his flashlight. Tempi Change Farms 2362 Seventh Line.
It would be about a half hour ride. Phillip had taught him the back roads
well, now he would pay for stealing the trunk. Tad smiled. It was so
easy. Hack bareback through the woods to the Seventh Line. Pick a nice
expensive saddle out of the tack room at Tempi Farms. Tack up and
gallop for home. He tucked the curly red hair of the wig behind his ears.
Adrienne Brooks was about to become very busy.

NINE

Jo Pilchard

By Monday evening Adrienne still didn't feel much like riding. Her left ear was still ringing and her head hurt when she tipped it to the side. She hadn't told anyone including T.J.. Adrienne's first Horse Trials of the year were on Sunday, and she didn't want her mother to be upset or make her withdraw her entry. T.J. could still tell that something was not quite right. Adrienne was far too quiet. T.J. worked Dakotaroo calmly back and forth over a single vertical jump in the centre of the ring, all the while keeping one eye out for Adrienne.

"I've been doing a lot of thinking about that picture," she said taking a break and walking Dakota on loose reins.

"*You've* been doing a lot of thinking! How about me! It's not me!"

"I know. I believe you. It's just that; Adrienne, that may be your horse."

Adrienne was still for a moment. She halted Annie on the rail and slouched down. T.J. thought for the first time in a long time, Adrienne was going to cry.

"I know," she said taking a deep breath. "I know Teej, someone is pretending to be me. Someone took Annie and is pretending to be me."

No one else ever rode Annie. Never, ever. T.J. was really unsure which was upsetting Adrienne more, that someone was impersonating her to get her into trouble, or that someone borrowed her beautiful horse.

"What can I do? I'll have to start sleeping in the barn. I mean, if someone can just walk in here, steal her, and then just bring her back… how can I protect her? I don't want her out of my sight right now. It's like I don't have a life. What am I supposed to do? She's the greatest horse in the world, I can't let it happen again. I can't sleep, I can't eat, I don't want to leave the farm…"

"Relax you big loser, it's not your horse." Phillip stood at the rail of the ring. "It's not you, not Annie, but yes, someone is trying to make people believe it's you." He held a blown up copy of the mysterious photograph in his right hand. "Here, the hoof on the near hind leg is white. I scanned the original photo and enlarged it 10 times. It's not Annie."

T.J. squinted at the picture. You could see the white hoof but there was no way to make out the face of the rider. "How come enlarging the photo makes it all blurry like that? You can't really tell anything from

71

that."

"The original was a bad printing of a photo taken by a cheap digital camera. The computer can only enlarge the pixels it gets. Sorry. At least it's not your horse. Dad would freak. Your pretty lucky he was out of town for this."

"But why? Why would anyone pretend to be me? I *always* just assume everyone wants to *be* me, but what would be the point of impersonating me?" Adrienne asked.

"To do something that only you are allowed to do?" T.J. suggested.

"To get you in trouble for doing something you're not allowed to do," said Phillip.

"Yeah, but why bother? Hooray! Adrienne is in trouble for riding across someone's property again. Big deal, I'm in trouble for doing that all the time."

Phillip's eyes met T.J.'s for a moment and then he looked at the ground. "I don't know," he said flatly. "Maybe it has nothing to do with you."

The girls had no sooner stopped talking to Phillip, than a black and white police cruiser pulled into the farm laneway. Constable Jo

Pilchard parked in front of the house, waved hello at the girls and went in to talk to Mrs. Brooks. At 29 years of age Jo Pilchard had worked for the Ontario Provincial Police for just over 5 years. When she first started her job, Jo soon figured out the best way to keep tabs on what all the locals were up to, was to make friends with a handful of the toughest kids. Phillip Brooks had been a challenge. Jo met him for the first time after he set fire to a portable toilet at the fair. He had filled the blue plastic porta-pottie high with newspaper, lit the paper on fire and closed the door. It was a rather impressive beacon in the dark. Phillip's rotten friends had turned him in, and Jo quickly realized the sooner she brought the kid with the quick mouth and the golden eyes under her wing, the safer all portable toilets would be.

"I wonder what's up now," said Adrienne.

"She wasn't carrying anything, at least she didn't have another picture of you and your horse wrecking stuff," laughed T.J.

"Or a big wanted poster for my arrest," Adrienne joked.

T.J. was worried, nothing about an official visit to Beaverbrook could possibly mean good news. T.J. dismounted, ran up her stirrups, loosened her girth and led Dakotaroo back to the barn with Adrienne and Annie not far behind.

"Your girlfriend Jo Pilchard is at the house talking to mom." Adrienne said walking past Phillip, "Aren't you going to go up and say hi?"

Phillip screwed up his face. "Um, no, it's O.K."

T.J. looked questioningly at him. She still thought of Jo as one of Phillip's favorite people in the whole wide world. He was always tracking down little bits of information for her, and running crazy errands. If he didn't want to say hello something must really be wrong. T.J. put Dakotaroo in the cross ties and quickly removed her saddle before searching for Phillip until she found him sitting quietly with Mr. Cyclops in the feed room. The orange and white cat had grown much fatter but still had one gross gooey eye.

"What's up? I thought you and Jo were friends?"

"Yeah, she's cool, I just don't want Tad to see me talking to her right now, so I'd better just stay here till she's gone."

"Do you have any idea why she's here? Do you think it has something to do with Tad and Bert Massey, or Laura Petty or even that fake picture of Adrienne? Do you think they're related?"

Phillip scratched Mr. Cyclops behind the ears and looked up at T.J. as if he was looking right through her. "I don't really want to talk about it right now." he said.

"Phillip c'mon," T.J. said waving her arms, "you ask for my help and then you get all clammed up! Is there a connection between Bert Massey's treasure and the fake picture of Adrienne?"

"I don't know," he said honestly, "I need more time to think. Adrienne's not really being much help, what's up with her?" he asked.

She bit her lower lip. "She's still hurting from crashing into the tree the other day. She doesn't want anyone to know. I can tell."

"Oh! Plane crash." Phillip said suddenly animated.

"What? Plane crash, what?" T.J. was very confused.

"That's how they died Teej. The Skyhouse people. They crashed their plane into a mountain someplace in Utah. There were actually *lots* of news stories about the crash on the internet. Mickey's dad was a big time criminal defense lawyer, and flew his private plane all over the place. I hope he was a better lawyer than he was a pilot."

"Phillip that's wonderful," T.J. stared at him wide eyed, as he looked back at her oddly. "Well, not really wonderful, actually very sad, but I am very glad you did the search for me. Was there anything about his mother? I don't even know her name."

"Tannis. Tannis Skyhouse, and she was 42 at the time of the crash."

"Tannis, my gosh that's such a nice name. Anything else?"

"Sorry Teej, anything else you're gonna have to ask for yourself."

T.J. held her hand up and looked closely at the ring. It's surface was etched with tiny scratches which reflected the light as if it were alive. Which of the tiny scratches had been made since T.J. owned it? Which were made before or even in the plane crash? You couldn't tell. "Thanks," she said quietly.

"Have you heard from Mickey lately?" asked Phillip. "Like, is he calling to ask how it's going with his freaky looking horse?"

T.J. shook her head, "He's traveling in Europe. Went to visit some relatives. That's partially why he sent Torque here for the first part of the summer, Mickey knew he wasn't going to be home to ride him anyhow."

"Torque's actually a pretty nice horse," said Phillip, " He's young, but you can tell he thinks about things, you can see it in his eyes. It's a cool thing about Appaloosa eyes, the white around the outside makes them look smarter."

Phillip watched from the feed room window as Jo's cruiser drove out the muddy lane, splashing in the puddles. The coast was clear. He fed Mr. Cyclops and brushed Robbie for awhile before walking slowly to the house, only to be met at the front door, by a very angry Arleen Brooks.

"Where were you yesterday?" she asked.

Phillip froze in his tracks and Adrienne crashed into him from behind as his momentum changed. "Um, exploring with Pez and Robbie that's all." Trying his best to stay as close to the truth as possible. Phillip pushed past her through the hallway, into the kitchen, grabbed a pop from the fridge and bounded up the stairs to his bedroom.

"Slow down, I need to talk to you both." Arleen hollered, she stopped for a moment and glanced at Adrienne. "Is it just me or is

Phillip particularly useless lately?"

Adrienne stole a spoonful cookie dough from a bowl on the counter. "Always useless, particularly useless lately. Tad has him doing some kinda secret work I think."

Arleen looked disapprovingly at Adrienne for a moment, "Secret paid work?"

"Gosh, I don't know. How am I supposed to know?" Adrienne exclaimed. "That would be between Tad and Loser Boy. I'm keeping out of it. What did constable Jo want?"

"That's exactly what I need to talk to you all about," Arleen said seriously. "There have been a number of saddles stolen from tack rooms on other farms. She wants us to be extra careful for the next little while. Lock the tack room, close the main gate at night. Four farms have been hit over the past week."

"Well, I guess it would be pretty easy to do, to steal saddles I mean. If the barn was really far away from the house you could just pull a truck up in the middle of the night and load up anything you want."

"Do you hear that Phillip?" Arleen hollered up the stairs, "Keep the tack room locked. Make sure all the little kids know to lock their lockers and make sure you let Tad know too for me, O.K?"

"Sure mom," Phillip grumbled back.

"Oh and Phillip," Mrs. Brooks said leaning on the railing of the stairs, "Jo Pilchard would like you to give her a call."

"O.K. what-ever," he replied.

"I worry about him. I wish your father was home more," said Arleen running her fingers through her short dark hair. "Phillip's spending way too much time creeping through the woods with Pez and the goat lately. I like the goat, but honestly, did you see what Phillip bought at the Massey auction? Old photos and a hat. What kind of kid buys old photos and a hat?"

"He's your kid Mom," Adrienne did not want to tell her mother about Phillip's secret sugar shack. There really wasn't much point. Adrienne just figured that the more time Phillip spent alone in his creepy shack the more time he wasn't bugging her or annoying her friends. "I think he'll be fine."

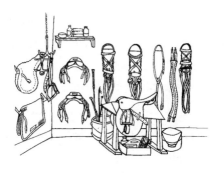

TEN

Meccano

Vinetyre Stables was a small training facility specializing in importing and quarantining horses from Germany. Tad had visited it the day before to scout the place out, pretending to be lost and asking for directions. Vinetyre fit Tad's criteria for a midnight raid, in that the barn was set well back in the lane, far away from the house. The feed room was the first door after a long row of stalls. The tack room was attached to the arena and doubled as the viewing lounge. Piece of cake. He walked Meccano silently up to the back door of the barn, dismounted and led the horse in. No one would hear a sound from the house, no one would see a thing. Once inside, his flashlight found the cross ties easily. Within minutes a lovely new saddle was on Meccano, Tad led him out of the barn, mounted, sent him forward and they were gone.

ELEVEN

The Trials of Adrienne

Adrienne and Animation had a lot of expectations to live up to. Last year Adrienne had been named to the Canadian Young Riders team, she was riding high, at the top of her game, Adrienne had become invincible. Drumlin Road Horse Trials would be the first competition of the year for Animation. Adrienne secretly wished that she had just one more week to train. Someone once told Adrienne it was way harder to stay at the top than get to the top. Today she understood exactly what they meant. There were plenty of other great young riders on fantastic horses, any one of them more than happy to bump Adrienne Brooks from the National Team.

It was extremely hot. Mrs. Brooks and T.J. trailered Annie over to the Trials with Adrienne. Tico Walsh, the coach of the Young Riders team would meet Adrienne and the other members there. Tico, an American was new to the team and T.J. learned a lot by watching them work. A thick humid haze hung over the grounds as they unloaded

Annie from the trailer. Mrs. Brooks, wearing a big goofy straw hat and a fanny pack, gathered up all of Adrienne's paperwork and set off towards the secretary's tent to pick up Annie's number. T.J. took the shipping wraps off the horse and began to tack her up, while Adrienne read over her dressage test for the 10 millionth time.

"They have decided that due to the heat, you are all permitted to ride your Dressage test without your jackets," Mrs. Brooks announced upon returning to the trailer. She passed the number 45 to T.J., who immediately put it on Annie's bridle so as not to lose it.

"I always wear my jacket. It's a five minute test, What kind of wimp do you have to be, not to be able to stand the heat for five measly minutes?" Adrienne said seriously.

"I know, just thought I'd let you know," said Arleen

T.J. smiled, Adrienne's jacket had a cool crest on it that distinguished her as being on the Canadian team and T.J. knew that Adrienne Brooks would happily wear that jacket all day long, every day if she could.

"I bought you a sandwich and a bottle of water at the snack bar," said Arleen. "It's here in the cooler bag in the truck, I knew you'd be hungry by now."

Adrienne was always hungry. Adrienne ate more food, without gaining weight than was humanly possible. Lots of riders couldn't eat before a big competition because of nerves. Being nervous just made

Adrienne talk faster, ride harder and eat more. She ate the sandwich, and downed the water without a second thought.

Tico met the team at the ring, Adrienne warmed up for Dressage, and then rode the most magnificent test T.J. had ever seen Annie do. A year of training had made a big difference in how Annie could carry herself and relax in the ring. Adrienne had also matured a lot in the past year, and took her detailed dressage work a whole lot more seriously. T.J. hauled two pails of water over to the trailer and waited for Adrienne to meet her back there. Adrienne returned looking strange.

"Wow, awesome test, I'm so impressed!" said T.J. "Do you want a drink of water?"

"Take her," said Adrienne abruptly.

"Sure, I set your cross country bridle out on the door and…"

"Take her," Adrienne dismounted and passed the reins to T.J., pushing past her in a hurry to get to the back of the trailer.

"What's up?"

Adrienne didn't answer.

T.J. quickly removed Annie's bridle and tied her to the trailer so the mare could eat her hay from the hay net. Behind the trailer she found Adrienne bent over at the waist with her hands on her knees, she had vomited and was as pale as a sheet of paper.

"Don't say a word; not to my mom, not to Tico, and definitely not to Phillip."

"Did you just puke?" asked T.J.

Adrienne gagged and vomited again.

"I guess that's a yes," T.J. said seriously. "Oh my, you're not still hurtin' from when you came off Torque are you? Adrienne, I feel so bad. Pull out of the cross country if your not 100%, everyone will understand."

"I'm fine, it's just the heat. Maybe that egg salad sandwich mom got me at the snack bar was bad, I don't know. I'll be fine in a minute." She was still bent over, her white gloves still on, "Where's the water?"

"Here," said T.J., "Let me take your jacket."

"Don't step there."

"Eeeww," T.J. smiled stepping over the puddle, "I wish I had a picture of you pukin' wearing your white pants and your team jacket. We could make a poster; Dressage, it's not for the weak!"

"Thanks. I'm glad someone finds this funny," Adrienne said slowly looking at her watch, "I've got to be ready to ride again in an hour." She took another drink from the water bottle. "I need your help T.J., I need to sit down for a while. Can you get Annie ready to go? You need to put the studs in her shoes and take out her braids. Jumping saddle on, breastplate, boots, you know my routine Teej, you can do it," Adrienne closed her eyes and fought off another wave of nausea. "I don't have much time to get feeling better."

"Pull out."

"No."

"Adrienne, it's dangerous."

"You're not my mom."

"She's gonna be back here any minute." T.J. warned.

"I'll be fine, get Annie ready," she looked at her watch again, "I'm to be in the start box at 1:25."

Arleen Brooks trundled over about 5 minutes later. She had a giant smile on her face. "They just posted the dressage scores," she said, "Adrienne your sitting in first place, way out in front. I'm so proud of how much you've improved. Everyone is so impressed."

The train sped across the dark, rolling countryside of northern England. Gray clouds hung low to the earth casting dark shadows to swallow the lonely herds of sheep. Mickey Skyhouse was not really great at traveling alone. There *were* times in his life when he desperately wanted to be by himself. After his parents first passed away, everyone he knew wanted him to spend time with them. His grandmother had smothered him with her attention. Now, only a little over a year later, the same people seemed to think the best thing for him to do would be to travel to see relatives in Europe, alone. He had sat on the airplane, over the Atlantic, with strangers.

The train would cross the border into Scotland in just over an hour. Mickey checked his watch and noticed a bald man, in the seat across from him, looking at his rings. Mickey wore them all now, all the time, just as his father had done until the day he died. Fifteen gold rings, all different, all signifying something important, on the hands of a long haired skinny kid traveling alone, far from home.

Every now and then the stainless steel train would speed past a small gathering of shaggy ponies. The ponies would lift their heads and prick their ears as the train approached, and then all but the very bravest would turn and run away. Outside Chorley, they passed a young girl waiting patiently on her horse for the train to pass through her village. The rider smiled and waved at the passengers on the train. Mickey waved back so excitedly, that he was more than a little embarrassed afterward. Something about the girl had reminded him of T.J.

Annie was very fresh, excited at her first time out for the year. Despite the heat, the haze, and humidity, she danced in the start box and began pulling hard from the moment they began. Adrienne took a deep breath and relaxed, *save your energy, don't fight the horse, it's a long, long course.*

T.J. and Mrs. Brooks sat where you could see quite a few of the jumps on course and listened to the announcer over the public address system to keep track of Adrienne's progress. "Animation #45 clear at the Hog's Back; Animation #45 clear at the Shark Tooth; Adrienne Brooks and Animation, our leaders after Dressage, clear at the Bank."

Mrs. Brooks looked at T.J. and smiled.

T.J. imagined Adrienne vomiting into the wind as she rode along.

Adrienne was about to pass out. It was so hot. Annie just kept leaning into the bridle and pulling for more. More speed, more height, more challenge, Adrienne couldn't be her match today, couldn't play her game. If the course sloped slightly uphill Annie would back off and Adrienne could ride out the storm, when they went downhill they fought about every stride. Something was about to give. There were 12 more fences left on the course, when Adrienne no longer had the strength to keep her precious balance and stay on.

"Animation #45, rider down at the Table."

It was a surprise to Mrs. Brooks, she wasn't really paying attention any more. Everything to that point had gone perfectly.

"Adrienne's down!" said T.J. grabbing Arleen by the arm and giving her a shake. "Adrienne's fallen off, we need to go now."

"Hold up. Rider down on course. Ambulance, can we have the Ambulance at jump #19, the table," the announcer boomed, "Could a representative of Adrienne Brooks please go to jump #19, the table, your rider is down."

T.J. and Mrs. Brooks ran hard across the open field to the far side of the course. Silence had fallen over the horse trials. A small crowd, including the ambulance, had gathered at the far side of the table. T.J. hopped over the small rope that marked the edge of the galloping lane and ran for the crowd.

"She just flew off as the mare was landing," a spectator called to T.J., "The horse didn't do anything wrong, she just flew right off!"

Animation was fine and being walked in a circle by Tico's assistant. Adrienne was still lying down on the ground.

"Hey you! Brooks' groom, take the horse will yah? Animation is fine, get her out of here while they look after Adrienne."

T.J. was a little bit stunned. Tico's assistant passed her Annie's reins and sent her on her way. "How's Adrienne?" she asked, "Is she O.K?"

"Stay back," someone yelled, "Get that horse out of here."

People were now purposely blocking the view of the crowd so they couldn't see the Medic working on Adrienne. T.J. couldn't see Arleen.

"Get that horse out of here!" someone hollered at her again.

T.J. turned and walked Animation back to the trailer. She should have told someone about Adrienne's fall off Torque a week ago. T.J. choked back tears and tried not to cry.

At the center of a circle of Horse Trials volunteers and curious onlookers Adrienne Brooks lay on the ground. She was the colour of dust and cold to the touch despite the heat. Tico was at her side trying to make her laugh and Arleen held her hand.

"I want the ambulance to take you to the hospital," said the Medic checking her vital signs for the second time.

"I'm fine, don't be silly, I'm fine. Mom, I'm good, let me get up, really."

"Kid, I know you, you're tough, you're hurtin' and your body is trying to tell you something. You're not listening kid, look at how much you're shaking."

Adrienne tried not to think of vomiting again and started to cry, "I'm fine, I'm just upset at myself, I, I usually win these things y'know."

"I know Brooks, but you're just a kid," he said taking her pulse. " Take it easy once in a while, I like all you riders in one piece." He felt her body over for injury, "you feel broken anywhere?" he asked.

"I don't break," she said.

The Medic smiled and shone a flashlight in her eyes. "Your head feel O.K? Which horse trials are we at today?"

"My head's great," Adrienne lied. "Drumlin Road. I practiced for it for 6 months, now let me go take care of my horse."

"You her mother?" the Medic asked Arleen.

"Yes."

"I really don't need to send her in the ambulance, but I would like her to visit the hospital today. Keep an eye on her, don't let her talk you into letting her do any rock climbing," he winked at Adrienne and gave her a hand to her feet.

The little crowd cheered loud enough for T.J. to hear them back at the trailer. She gave Annie a big hug and sighed in relief. Someone had to be looking out for Adrienne.

TWELVE

The Adrienne Wig

Phillip was home alone when Jo Pilchard came to call. Jo came on her own time, in her own car, and wearing her own clothes. Phillip had not returned her phone calls or e-mails in over 3 weeks, and someone was stealing saddles by the dozen from nearby farms. It was time to pay him a visit. She caught him off guard.

"Hey there!" she said smiling as he opened the door.

"Oh. Hi Jo. Mom's not here. Adrienne got dumped at Drumlin Road today, mom took her to the hospital. I think they're gonna keep her there for the night. Notice the peace and quiet around here?"

Jo looked shocked, "No way! Is she O.K?"

"Yeah, she's been throwing up all day, so she's all dehydrated or something. Mom figures she'll be out by morning."

"Thank goodness, and the horse is O.K?"

"Yup."

Jo placed her hand on the porch door, june bugs were stuck all over the screen and buzzed against the porch light, "It's actually you I came by to see Phillip," she said warmly, "Can I come in, or do I have to stay out here with the giant bugs?"

Phillip took a deep breath, "Sure thing Jo, what's up?" He led her to the kitchen and offered her two oatmeal cookies. Food made everything better.

"Saddles are still going missing from riding stables all over this area. It's a little like when Dakotaroo went missing, the O.P.P. have more important work to do than worry about saddles. It's not a case my supervisors want me to spend much time on, but horse people are my friends, and I want to help out any way I can." she paused, " I was hoping you'd want to help me figure this one out."

Phillip had a lot of trouble resisting the urge to join in. He decided to play detective, as long as she didn't make him talk about Tad. " I don't know, Jo"

"You don't know, or you know something you'd rather not tell me?"

He smiled. "Don't just assume stuff. I don't know. I don't know anything," he paused, walked into his mothers office, and returned with the strange picture of someone pretending to be Adrienne, "but I do have this,"

Jo looked at the picture and shook her head, "Is this Adrienne?"

"It's someone pretending to be Adrienne. Someone disguised themselves as Adrienne and rode across the golf course at the Country Club after midnight three weeks ago. It freaked her out big time."

Jo squinted at the picture. "So it's *not* Adrienne?"

"Nope. Her clothes, her hair, not her."

"Wow, this *is* interesting."

T.J. returned home from the hospital when visiting hours were done. She had put her paddock boots on at 7:30 that morning, before taking Adrienne to the Horse Trials, and was taking them off for the first time at 10:30 p.m. She had washed her face and put the kettle on for a cup of tea, before her mother even noticed she was there.

"Theresa, you're home!" her mother said cheerfully, "How's Adrienne?"

"She's good, I think. She figures she just ate a bad egg sandwich or has stomach flu or something. They just kept her overnight to try and get some fluids into her."

"Thank goodness, I'm so glad you guys are always there for each other. It's nice, I'm proud of you T.J."

T.J. didn't feel all that proud of herself. She had kept Adrienne's fall from Torque and her throwing up before riding cross-country a secret. It had been a really long, stressful day. Not much could have made it worse.

Mrs. Thompson gave her a kiss on the head and started up the stairs to go to bed. "Oh, T.J., I almost forgot," she turned and smiled, "Mickey called tonight from Scotland, he just wanted to say hello."

It was so hot that the wig was making his head itch badly. The humidity of the day had carried over into the evening without a sign of breaking. Everything was silent and still, as Tad and Meccano quietly walked the rail trail in the dark. He had collected saddles from eight different farms over the past 3 weeks, once as many as three in a night. He had enough now; easily enough, to sell and repay Laura Petty the five thousand dollars she had paid him for finding that dumb trunk of Bert Massey's. Five thousand now, five thousand when she safely received the treasure. Stupid metal trunk, he knew Phillip had hidden it someplace, he'd just have to be patient and wait the kid out. Phillip would crack, he'd brag about it to one of the other kids at the barn soon enough. It was only a matter of time before he'd be asking Tad to help him open the darn thing. For now, Tad had treasure of his own. He adjusted the wig again and tried not to laugh out loud.

Constable Jo Pilchard received her first good lead about the missing saddle case, early the next morning. The owner of Spruce Hill

Arabians, Prentice Howard, called in a panic. A saddle, a championship cooler and 4 horse shipping boots had gone missing from their tack room last night. All the equipment was custom made, sentimental and irreplaceable. In the spring, Spruce Hill had installed small cameras in the stalls to watch the mares carefully and see if they needed help with foaling. Small high tech cameras, specially designed to work in the dark.

"She's not a very clever girl that kid," Prentice fumed, "She's going to pay dearly for this. This is a small, close knit, horse community, and she has just gone *too* far. No one will ever let that spoiled brat on their property again. I want you to know right now, that I have a lot of friends in *very* high places in this provincial government. I want this young girl to go to jail for this! What kind of cruel joke does she think she's been playing? So many people have been hurt by what she's done…" Prentice rambled on and on as though she never needed to take a breath.

"Who?" said Jo interrupting, although the answer really didn't come as a surprise.

"That Brooks girl," she spat, "the one with all the red hair. Adrienne Brooks. We have her on video."

How could Adrienne Brooks possibly be in the hospital and stealing saddles at the same time? Constable Jo met with Prentice Howard that afternoon to tour the crime scene and watch the video tape.

The thief had left nothing behind, no tire tracks, no finger prints, only hoof prints in the dirt mixed in with the hundreds of other hoof prints on the farm.

"She rides in on her horse," said Prentice. "She rides in on bareback, puts her horse in the cross-ties, tacks up with a new saddle and then rides away. Look at her! Look how cocky she is. She acts as if no one would ever suspect it was her in a million years."

The figure on the video worked slowly and moved through the barn with ease. The horses in the stalls stayed calm and everything was quiet.

Jo Pilchard smiled seriously. "Prentice, it's not Adrienne Brooks."
"It is so! I know that girl. Tall, bushy red hair, rides a tall dark bay mare."

Jo rewound the video tape and watched it again in slow motion as she replied. "Adrienne took a fall at Drumlin Road Horse Trials yesterday, they kept her in the hospital overnight for observation. The kid in the video is cocky because she is not Adrienne." Jo froze the image on the face of the thief as it turned towards the camera. It was dark and blurry and still impossible to see.

HARDWARE

Sunlight shone through the vertical slits between the dry barn boards. Dust sparkled, suspended in the yellow beams of light. Tad had been there, in the hay loft of Bert Massey's barn, Phillip could tell. Much of the hay had been moved aside since he had searched for the horse collar, and the large sliding doors were now closed on the granary. Phillip crept without a sound across the packed straw on the floor and pushed the door open. Although it did offer up a small squeal of objection, it rolled surprisingly well on its rusted steel rollers. Phillip stepped cautiously inside and waited patiently for his eyes to adjust to the light. Throughout the rectangular room, piled carefully on stacked bales of hay were displayed 12 beautifully expensive English saddles. Stubbens, Passiers, Schleese, Keiffer, at least one of each, many of some. Phillip shuddered. *The Saddle Thief. Tad is the Saddle Thief.* He *had* been the one pretending to be Adrienne. Tad was the Saddle Thief, and Phillip had found his lair. He should have known. It was so easy. No one kept track of Tad, and since the auction no one had set foot in the Massey barn.

Phillip quickly walked around the granary, and surveyed Tad's work. There would be way over 20,000 dollars worth of stolen items there. Tad was going to be in big trouble if he got caught. Chills crept up Phillip's spine, and made the hairs stand up on the back of his neck. Tad was going to be in big trouble if he got caught, and Phillip could turn him in. He needed to get out of there. He needed to get out of there now. Slowly he backed away from the saddles and reached for the door. Phillip's hand suddenly touched something soft and furry, and had knocked it to the floor. There, on the narrow wooden planks of the granary floor was Adrienne's hair. Tad's Adrienne wig laid there like a curly auburn dead animal. It gave Phillip the creeps so badly, that he had to use a stick to pick it up and hang it back on the wall. His heart was pounding. *Run! Run away now. Go far, get away from what you know. Go now.* He scrambled across the straw, flew down the wide wooden staircase, and forgetting about the missing bottom step, he fell hard to his knees on the cold concrete below.

"Ahhh!" he let out a yell. The palms of his hands were scratched and bleeding from trying to break his fall.

Robbie raised his head and bleated in reply.

"Shhh!" Phillip hushed him. Scrambling to his feet, he quickly untied Robbie from the rusted metal cow stanchions. "Listen," he said. "We have to run."

Phillip ran like a maniac, leading Robbie through the back of Bert Massey's farm. He was through the furthest field, and at the edge of the rail trail before he dared to stop and catch his breath. Standing in the safety of the trees, he looked back at the old brown barn and the secret it held. Suddenly the sweat on his brow became cold and he cursed. He was scared, his palms hurt and he had forgotten to close the granary door.

HARDWARE

"I have asked your mother to keep you off your horse for a while," the young doctor told Adrienne as he shone a tiny flashlight into her right eye. "Look up please. Yes," he smiled as he wrote some illegible notes on her chart. "I'd like you to come back to the hospital for some tests this week."

"No way! No riding? C'mon!"

"Your mom say's you've taken a few good falls lately, and from all the spectator accounts, you did pass out while on course yesterday. We all just want to make sure you're in shape to keep competing, O.K?" The young doctor held a clipboard in his left hand and continued to make notes on Adrienne's chart without looking at her.

"I'm *fine* you know. Really. This is all just a big waste of time."

"Adrienne," said her mother, "you have a whole summer ahead of you. Co-operate please."

"You can stay home and take it easy, or you can stay here where we can watch you. It's your choice Adrienne."

THIRTEEN

Skeleton Key

The phone in her office rang a painstaking 6 times before Jo Pilchard's voicemail answered the call. "You have reached the personal and confidential voicemail of…" Phillip really didn't know what to do, "If this is an emergency you can call the Ontario Provincial Police radio room at …" Phillip didn't want to discuss the case with anyone else. Jo knew the girls, Jo would understand and forgive him for keeping some details from her. Phillip firmly pressed "1" on his phone as instructed, and left her a message.

"Hey Jo, it's Phillip Brooks calling, please come by the farm when you get a chance. I, um, I could really use your help right now," he put the phone down and tried not to feel like the message was too pathetic.

Phillip grabbed a handful of Fruit Loops from the kitchen, slipped on his boots and went out to the barn to check on Robbie. Robbie *had* looked freakishly unhealthy since Laura Petty had left town, but he was much worse today. Tad hated him. Phillip was now beginning to suspect that Tad somehow knew more about Robbie than he was letting on. Maybe someone or something was poisoning Robbie. Maybe Robbie was *supposed* to die, that's why Laura Petty told Phillip *exactly* where to bury him if he did. Maybe Laura paid Tad to keep an eye on the goat as well as the trunk. But why? Phillip started to run toward the barn, he flung open the door, ran through the aisle with his heart pounding in his ears. Robbie lay, just barely alive, in the middle of the feed room floor.

About an hour later, veterinarian Ed Marshall had arrived at the Brooks' to answer Phillip's emergency call. Arleen Brooks and Phillip were doing their best to keep Robbie comfortable. Dr. Marshall was approaching 50. He was short, stocky and more than just a little bit bald. Although he had been to the Brooks' farm before, he was not their usual vet, and specialized in treating ruminants like sheep, goats and cattle.

"And, who do we have here?" asked Dr. Marshall picking up Robbie's chin from the hay and opening his eyelids to look at his pupils.

"Robbie," replied Phillip, his hand shaking as he stroked Robbie softly. "I think he's been poisoned doctor. Please don't let him die."

"Poisoned Phillip, really," said Arleen, "he eats a lot of junk."

Phillip tried hard not to cry. Mr. Cyclops brushed up against his leg and purred for attention.

"We should look after that eye too while I'm here," the

veterinarian added nodding in the direction of the gooey looking cat. He put on two surgical gloves and knelt down beside Robbie, "He has a strange shape Phillip. His belly, we call it his rumen, it's really big. Otherwise he's quite lean, he's not fat at all." The veterinarian poked and prodded at Robbie's belly until the goat bleated in opposition. "Has he been uncomfortable for a while?"

"Yes," said Phillip quietly, "he's just always a little bit uncomfortable, he can never find a comfy spot to lie down, but he eats like crazy. I just figured he couldn't be feeling all that bad if he still had a big appetite. The last two days though, it's been different. He's been just lying around a whole lot more. It's like he's giving up or something."

Dr. Marshall asked Phillip to place a clean horse blanket down on the concrete floor of the barn. They then carefully rolled Robbie onto the blanket and on to his right side.

"I'll need some hot water Phillip," said the vet handing him a shiny stainless steel pail. "Seems like a there's a lot of excitement going on around here lately. You O.K.?"

"Yeah, so far," replied Phillip. His face was all puffy and red from crying but he was beginning to feel better.

"I'm going to have to cut Robbie open to save him. Are you going to be alright if you see the inside of your friend here?" Dr. Marshall asked kindly while injecting the goat with a sedative.

101

"Cool," sniffed Phillip, "I'd love to see the inside of Robbie. That's awesome."

"Good then."

Dr. Marshall took a small pair of electric clippers, and removed a large patch of the goat's hair from the left side of his belly. He then washed the smooth, shaved belly with warm water and some foamy red surgical soap. He put on a clean pair of thin blue latex gloves and passed a pair to Phillip.

"Here," he said. "Put those on in case I need your help. Try to keep them clean, he's nice and sleepy now so you shouldn't have to hold him down at all."

The vet made small injections with a needle along the length of the shaved patch to freeze the area he was about to cut. He began the incision with a razor sharp scalpel and cut a slit in Robbie's skin just long enough for his hand to fit through. There was very little blood.

A small crowd of riding students and their parents began to gather around Robbie's operation. Some people stood and watched, kids sat on the hay bales. Apparently Robbie's misfortune was proving to be quite entertaining.

Dr. Marshall cut through Robbie again. This time he made a deep incision inside the first one. "Now," he said to Phillip, "Now, we're inside Robbie's rumen. It's like a big vat of chewed up food. Bacteria and other microbes live here and help the goat digest roughage like hay." The veterinarian stuck his hand up inside Robbie and pulled out a handful of very foul smelling green mush. "See, if Robbie was poisoned and the microbes all died, he would probably die too. I can give him some stuff to rebuild his microbial population if we caught this in time."

"Wow," said Phillip wide-eyed, "He has a population living inside him!"

"Yeah, you do too. He just has way more little creatures in his belly. They help him digest leaves and things."

"I do? Eeeeewww."

"I don't think that's our problem here though." Dr. Marshall was now almost elbow deep inside of Robbie and seemed to be fishing around for something. "Ooooo," he said, "I'll have to make this incision bigger."

"What's wrong," asked Phillip alarmed.

The vet made the hole into Robbie almost twice as big.

"This," he said. And reaching his hand in once again, he pulled out a very large smelly mass of gooey silver metal.

Phillip cradled the mass of steaming, foul smelling metal in his two gloved hands and stared at it in disbelief.

"What is *this*?" he asked.

"Treasure," joked the veterinarian, "we call it hardware. Sometimes a ruminant eats a piece of metal, and it stays stuck in them for a long time. Put it in the pail to wash off and we'll see what he had."

Phillip placed the "hardware" in the pail and stirred it around while Dr. Marshall sewed Robbie up. "I can't believe he ate something that big," he said.

"Oh, he didn't eat it all at once," laughed the doctor looking into the pail. "I think if you look at it carefully you'll find there's a magnet in the center. Somebody fed him the magnet on purpose so the metal would stick to it."

"That's weird."

"Yes, it is for a goat. Cattle are fed magnets all the time to catch the metal they eat. Robbie is really far too small to be carrying around a big cow sized chunk of hardware like that."

Phillip was fascinated by the ball of metal. There were bits of wire, horseshoe nails, a piece of a Hot Wheel car, a thumb tack, something that looked oddly like an earring and even a long canister, the size of Phillip's finger, that looked like it was made of real silver.

"Can I keep it?" he asked.

"Of course Phillip, its all yours. Robbie should be fine now. I'll put him on some medication for a week, O.K?" Dr. Marshall looked over at Phillips treasure. "I wonder if there's anything inside that metal canister."

Phillip peeled the canister away from Robbie's treasure ball. He

104

twisted it in two directions at the center. It was smooth, shiny and bright, and came apart in two beautiful pieces. Inside was a slender, silver, skeleton key.

FOURTEEN

Phillip Brooks

It was just after dinner when Adrienne answered the door in her pyjamas. Jo Pilchard, in uniform, carrying a stack of papers and video tapes, greeted her smiling.

"Hey Adrienne, how are you!"

"I'm fine. Doctor grounded me from riding and wants me to go in for some scans of my head or something evil. But I'm O.K." Adrienne let Jo into the house and followed her to the kitchen. "What's up?"

"Um, I need to talk to you, but you probably want your mom present." Jo replied.

"Sounds bad," said Adrienne.

"No, not really," said Jo cautiously, "I just think it would be easier for everyone if I only had to explain this whole thing once. Is Phillip around?"

Adrienne winced, "Yeah, his dumb goat friend almost died today, mom and Phillip just went to the barn to check on him, they'll be back in a minute. Would you like a cup of tea?"

"Sure," said Jo. Phillip and Arleen could be heard making noise while taking off their boots in the mud room.

Phillip was obviously relieved to see that the police officer had received his call. "Thanks for coming Jo," he said.

"I was on my way anyhow," she replied warmly, " Something came up today that I need to discuss with Adrienne." Jo turned to Adrienne and became serious, "I have something I need to show you. You're not in trouble or anything, I just need you to know what's going on, and how you can help the police. If you're not feeling O.K., then let me know, and I'm sure your mom, Phillip and I can work this out together."

"I'm fine," Adrienne replied and then hesitated for a moment. "Can I call T.J. to come over, if you need my help you'll need her help too."

"Sure," smiled Jo.

Phillip looked uncomfortable the whole time Adrienne was on the phone with T.J. He desperately wanted to tell the police officer what he had found in the barn but was still afraid of Tad.

"I need to show you a video tape I received today. Is there a place where we can watch it?"

"Yes," said Arleen. "Please, come sit in the living room."

Jo loaded the tape into the player. "This is going to come as quite a surprise," she warned, "It was taken last night at Spruce Hill Arabians on a special camera to monitor nighttime foalings. The quality of the image is quite poor. I'll run the whole tape through once, and then we can all watch it again slowly. I need your help to try to identify who in the world this girl is."

The tape began slowly, soon in the dark a tall figure appeared, black riding pants, lime green Tipperary body protector, wild red fuzzy hair sticking out from under a black riding helmet. She led a dark bay horse with lime green polo wraps through the barn. They all watched in silence as the thief worked in the darkness. Horse in the cross-ties, saddle on the horse. Adrienne felt sick to her stomach again but was afraid to say so. Phillip squirmed

"Sorry Adrienne, I know this must be pretty hard to watch," said Jo, "Any idea who she might be?"

"No, but someone's in big trouble," said Adrienne furious.

Phillip got up and walked to the window. He pressed his fingertips to the cool glass and looked out into the darkness.

"Phillip?" asked Jo, "What's wrong?"

"It's Tad, Tad Dillon," he said quietly. "He's dressing up as Adrienne and stealing saddles to punish me for keeping Bert Massey's treasure from him. I found them today," he turned from the window and looked at them seriously. "I know where they all are. That's why I called you this morning Jo. I found where Tad is keeping the stolen

108

saddles."

"Great! Why didn't he dress up as *you* and steal stuff from the neighbours?"

"He's tall, no one would have ever believed it was me anyhow," Phillip replied.

"Bert Massey had a treasure?" said Arleen. "Why do you kids always have these stupid secret adventures going on behind my back?"

"Phillip, how do you know it's Tad Dillon. Can you *prove* it's him?"

Phillip was quiet for a moment. Everyone stared at him waiting for his reply.

"No," he said finally, "I know it's him though. He took me to break into Bert Massey's house 2 months ago. That's where the saddles are, in the granary in Bert's barn. His curly wig and Adrienne costume are there too, I saw them."

"Oooo... I hate that Tad guy so much," said Adrienne.

"And how do you know Tad Dillon, Phillip," asked Jo, beginning to take notes on a small pad of paper.

"He boards his horse with us," Arleen answered for Phillip. "Tad moved in after Laura Petty left for Palm Springs. He's 18, his parents manage a resort in Bermuda, and have a home in Caledon. This year they left him alone here in Canada to finish up high school, and continue to show his horse. He has a very nice horse."

"He's a jerk," said Phillip.

"I hate him," seethed Adrienne.

"O.K, great, the guy's a jerk and you hate him. We still have to prove it was *him* on the video," said Jo. "I'm gonna hop in the car and take a trip over to the Massey Farm right now. I'll be back soon," she continued to take notes as she spoke. "Please, whatever you do, do not confront Mr. Dillon about anything we have discussed this evening." she looked seriously at Adrienne, "It's important that this Tad guy carry on stealing things like normal until we have built enough of a case against him." She stopped writing for a moment and put the end of her pen in her mouth, "What *is* 'Tad' short for anyway?"

Suddenly, there was a knock at the front door.

"It's just T.J.," said Arleen rising to her feet, I'll let her in.

The young man at the door took her quite by surprise. He wore a black leather jacket, blue jeans and light brown cowboy boots. His long straight hair was cut to the length of his shoulders and tucked neatly behind his ears. Both hands were in his pockets.

"C-an I help you?" asked Arleen slowly, "Has your car broken down on the road or something?"

The young man smiled shyly. "No ma'am," he said, "I'm Michael Skyhouse."

FIFTEEN

Mickey Skyhouse

"Mickey!" Adrienne squealed running to the front door.

"Hey," said Mickey waving.

"You're here!"

"Um, yeah. I got a little homesick for horses while I was traveling. I made a little detour, if that's O.K."

"Of course it's O.K.," said Arleen, "Come on in, it's very nice to finally meet you. Jo, Phillip, this is Mickey Skyhouse, T.J. and Adrienne's friend from Montana."

Jo had already risen from the couch and was preparing to leave. Mickey offered his hand for the officer to shake. It was not surprising to him that the constable was there, her police car was parked out in front of the house after all, it just seemed as if he had walked into the middle of something rather important.

"Be careful," said Phillip, "there are no lights upstairs in the barn."

"Thanks buddie," said Jo smiling as she laced up her boots, "I'll

111

be fine."

Everyone was quiet for a moment.

"Have I come at a bad time?" asked Mickey.

"No," said Arleen, "Jo is going out in the dark to find some stolen property, Phillip is just about to tell us all about Bert Massey's treasure, Adrienne is ready to punch someone, and T.J. is on her way over here right now," she passed him a cup of tea, "I think your timing is just excellent."

It was silver and sparkled as he turned it round and round in his fingers, "It was inside Robbie all along," he began. "I think Laura Petty hid it there. She fed it to Robbie, locked in a capsule and attached to a magnet. It wouldn't have been too difficult to do. She just had to hide the capsule in a doughnut or something."

Adrienne tipped her head to the side, "Is it a key?" she asked.

"Yes," said Phillip smiling mischievously. "It's the key to Bert Massey's treasure."

"So, who *is* this Bert guy?" asked Mickey holding his mug of tea in both hands and sipping from it slowly.

"An old neighbour," said Arleen, "He lived alone on the Fourth Line."

"He's dead now," added Adrienne.

"...and Bert had a treasure?" Mickey continued still looking confused.

"He had *lots* of treasures, he had traveled the world collecting cool things when he was young. They auctioned off most of his stuff weeks ago. Antiques, fossils, paintings, it was amazing. Tad knew about Bert's most valuable possession and stole it from his house just before the auction. I was with him when he tried to take it from the farm. It's in a really heavy old metal trunk. I don't think Tad wanted me around when he tried to open it, so he left it hidden in the barn." Phillip looked embarrassed for a moment. "I went back the next day with Pez and stole it back for Bert."

"Bert's dead Phillip. Why would you need to steal his stuff back for him?" questioned Adrienne.

"Because it was the right thing to do?" asked Mickey.

"Because Bert was my friend," said Phillip.

Arleen took a closer look at Phillip's key. "So this key opens the trunk?"

"I'm pretty sure." Phillip paused and held the key up to the light, "I should get a chance to check tomorrow."

There was a knock at the door.

"That should be T.J." said Arleen.

"Or Jo," said Phillip.

"Or Tad," smiled Adrienne. "He's coming to get you Phillip."

"Dressed as you I hope! This I gotta see," he laughed.

"Kids, stop." Arleen scolded, "This is serious."

113

T.J. let herself in the door after knocking. "Hello, it's Teej!" she yelled.

"C'mon in." hollered Adrienne, "we're in the living room, we've got company."

T.J. wore an old wool sweater her grandma had knit for her dad, on top of a t-shirt and overalls. The sleeves of the sweater covered her hands so only her finger tips stuck out from the wooliness. Her blonde hair was pulled back into a messy pony-tail with lots of hair bits sticking out. She froze at the living room door.

"Careful now, that may be Tad dressed as T.J." Phillip cautioned sarcastically.

T.J. raised her fingers to her mouth.

"Hey Teej," said Mickey.

She slowly entered the room, sat down on a chair across from Mickey and stared at him squinting. "Hey," she said, "You cut your hair."

"Yeah," he laughed, "it's nice to see you too."

"Sorry…I just…I was trying to figure out what was different and…"

"O.K., that's definitely not Tad," said Phillip.

"T.J., Phillip's found the missing saddles. He's sure it's Tad that's been stealing them from the neighbours but we have no proof." Adrienne added.

"Jo Pilchard has a video of someone disguised as Adrienne breaking into Spruce Hill Arabians last night."

Mickey took another sip of his tea. "So this Tad guy stole Bert Massey's treasure *and* a bunch of saddles."

"Dressed as Adrienne don't forget, that's the freaky part," said Phillip.

"O.K., dressed as Adrienne," added Mickey, "Why?"

Phillip looked puzzled, "Why steal the saddles, or why dress as Adrienne?"

"Both," answered Adrienne.

T.J. remained motionless.

"He needed money," said Phillip. "Laura Petty had paid him big bucks to find Bert Massey's trunk and he lost it. I'm pretty sure he wanted to find a way to punish me for taking the trunk, so he decided to frame Adrienne for stealing saddles. Everyone knows Adrienne, every horseperson in the county has seen her and Annie galloping all over the place. The biggest mistake Tad made was actually thinking *I cared* if Adrienne was in trouble."

"Gee thanks Phillip," said Adrienne.

"We watched the video with Jo before you got here Teej, with a wig on Tad really makes a lovely Adrienne," Phillip added.

"How long are you here Mickey? Where are you staying?" asked T.J. finally.

115

He tucked his hair back behind his right ear, "I'm to meet Uncle Den in Connecticut next Tuesday for an interview at school. I have a flight from Toronto to Hartford booked for Tuesday morning. Until then I'm pretty much on my own. I thought I could come and see Torque, hang out with you guys for a week and sleep in the barn if I needed to."

"You're *not* sleeping in the barn Michael," said Arleen, "Phillip would be more than happy to have you share his room."

"It's O.K.," he said "I don't mind staying in the barn, as long as I can get cleaned up before I have to leave on Tuesday." he winked at T.J.

"No way," Arleen replied, "With all the strange things going on around here I'm sure we'll all sleep a lot better if you're in the house."

"Yeah, you can sleep in my bed, then when Tad comes to attack me for squealing to the cops about him, he can accidentally beat the snot out of you instead!" Phillip smiled.

"Um, great." Mickey smiled.

"Tuesday," said T.J.

"I think you're going to be very pleased with Torque. He's jumping really well," said Adrienne. "We can go out on a long hack tomorrow. If we ride to the McLaughlin farm you can take some of the cross-country fences there. He's *very* cool to work with."

"Adrienne," Arleen said sternly. "you are *not* riding anywhere."

Adrienne closed her eyes tightly and made a groaning sound. "Awww..shoot. Sorry Mom, I forgot."

"Adrienne's been grounded from riding by the doctor," T.J. explained seriously.

Mickey looked concerned ,"You O.K?" he asked.

"Yup, took a couple a good falls lately, everyone just wants me to take it easy for a week or so. I'm fine."

Jo Pilchard called from the Massey Farm and spoke to Arleen as the girls took Mickey out for a tour of the barn. The stolen property was all there, in the granary as Phillip had said, but there was still no real evidence to pin the crime on Tad Dillon. Jo and another officer were going to stay the night at the old barn and set up a stake out. When Tad returned for his stolen goods, they would be ready to arrest him. The whole operation may take a few days to be done properly, she warned Arleen. In the meantime, she could not stress enough how important it was that everyone, including Arleen and Mr. Brooks, not confront Tad about the missing saddles or the video of imposter Adrienne.

"It's O.K. Jo," said Arleen, "Phillip, despite all his joking around, is really too frightened of Tad to want to talk to him, and Adrienne is taking the week off from riding. I'll make sure to tell the kids, if Tad comes by to ride his horse, they are just to carry on as if *nothing* was going on. Everything around here should be nice and quiet for awhile."

Tad Dillon came to Beaverbrook Hall early the next evening. It was suddenly very cold for the month of June.

Mickey and T.J. were riding back along the road from the McLaughlin's farm when Tad's silver Honda passed them.

"That's him," said T.J., "That's Tad's car, we'd better hurry."

Phillip was alone in the barn with Robbie when the Honda pulled in the lane. He wore the key to Bert Massey's trunk under his shirt, on a chain around his neck. Adrienne was in the house watching T.V.. Mrs. Brooks had gone out to get groceries, but had left her cell phone with Phillip. He was to call Jo Pilchard immediately the instant Tad showed up at the stables. As Tad stepped out of the car, Phillip quickly dialed her number.

Tad wore dark sunglasses so you couldn't see his eyes. "Hey, Phil, who's the dirt farmer riding with Theresa Thompson?" he yelled into the barn.

Phillip had accidentally dialed the number wrong. Tad was walking toward him. There was no time to try it again. Jo would have to wait.

"Hi Tad," said Phillip, his voice wavering "Um, it's T.J.'s imaginary boyfriend from Montana, y'know, the guy that owns the horse."

"I thought that guy was rich or something, he looks like a loser. Who wears cowboy boots?" Tad spat.

"People from Montana do I think," said Phillip, *try to act as normal as possible,* he thought to himself. Tad was acting normal.

118

Normal like a jerk.

Tad looked around the barn to make sure they were alone before checking his watch. "I'm in a bit of a hurry today Phillip," he said. "Can we talk for a minute? 'Cause you see, I think you know what happened to that big green trunk that came out of the old Hermit's house. I needed that trunk, that's why I moved it out of the house, I needed it then and I need it now."

Phillip slowly walked to the door of the barn and tried to make it look as if he were wandering outside. He picked up a broom and started to sweep the concrete pad at the front of the barn. Maybe Adrienne would see him, maybe his mom would drive in the lane. "I don't know Tad," Phillip lied, "I told you before, I don't know what happened to that trunk." His hands were shaking, he gripped the broom and swept harder.

"You're lying," laughed Tad, "You're the worst liar I have ever met."

The cell phone in Phillip's pocket rang. He had to think for a minute about what he should do and then decided to answer it. It was Adrienne calling from the house.

"Yes." Tad heard him say. "Yes, please, yes."

Adrienne was on her way.

"Who was that?" asked Tad.

"Adrienne," said Phillip, "She's in the house and she wanted to know if I would like a sandwich." He lied a little better this time.

Tad grabbed Phillip by the collar and dragged him back into the barn. The broom crashed to the ground. Tad pushed him up against the wall and held him there.

"Listen you little nerd, you don't know who you're dealing with here, I need the trunk and I need it today." Tad squashed Phillip hard enough, that the tack hooks on the wall were poking into his rib cage.

"I can't breathe Tad, stop!" said Phillip loudly.

"Tell me where you took the trunk!"

Adrienne is on her way, Phillip thought. *Adrienne is calling Jo and she's on her way.*

It was then that Tad first noticed the key hanging around Phillip's neck. "Hey! You have the key. I saw that key when Laura first took it from the old Hermit dude. That's the key to the trunk."

Phillip was still being flattened by Tad. *How long can it possibly take for Adrienne to call Jo, get her boots on and walk here from the house?*

Tad tore the key and chain from around Phillip's neck.

"Owwwww!"

"You won't be needing this, and if you won't tell me where trunk is, I guess I'll just have to find it myself. It doesn't matter *now* does it Phillip. I have the key. It's just a matter of time till I find the stupid trunk. No one can stop me now Phillip, no one." Tad put Phillip down and turned to leave.

Adrienne Brooks stood silently in the doorway.

"Are you going someplace Tad?"

Tad swallowed, "I'm in a bit of a hurry Adrienne, if you can just step aside, I have something very important to do."

"Going to check on your saddles." Adrienne purred.

"What?" said Tad angrily.

"You know, the stolen, missing saddles that everyone in the county has been looking for." Adrienne's eyes narrowed to slits, "How dare you try to pin this on me!"

"Just doing business Adrienne, he said pushing past her. Besides," he said, "it's really just small potatoes. All those people have insurance, they'll have new saddles in no time." Tad smiled flashing his perfect teeth, "I love robbing from the rich."

"Oh, that's just wonderful, and I get the reputation for breaking into barns and stealing stuff."

"You had a reputation for causing trouble anyway. You're reckless Adrienne. Reckless, and not even a very good rider."

Adrienne then did something she never imagined anyone would ever make her angry enough to do. Adrienne Brooks, all 5 foot 11 inches and 125 pounds of her, hauled off and punched Tad Dillon square in the face.

Tad reeled. He rocked from side to side with both of his hands covering his nose, and then yelling loudly, stretched out both arms and pushed Adrienne hard to the floor. Adrienne fell with a thud and rolled away so as not to get hit again.

"Stay down!" yelled Tad.

Adrienne had no intention of getting up. She stayed quietly in the corner with her head in her hands. Apparently punching Tad was not the best idea she had ever had.

"Don't hurt her!" screamed Phillip raising his hands to his ears. "The trunk..." he blurted, "the trunk is in the old sugar shack at the back of Bert Massey's farm."

"Thanks pal," said Tad sarcastically, throwing the key into the air and catching it again. "Now I have absolutely everything I need. Way to go Adrienne."

Tad ran to his Honda just as Constable Jo Pilchard pulled into the laneway in her police car.

T.J. and Mickey rode into the yard, and dismounted. It was Mickey who noticed Adrienne on the ground first.

"What makes you think you'll get away with any of this?" Adrienne yelled at Tad defiantly, trying to disguise how physically horrible she was feeling.

Leaving their horses, Mickey and T.J. raced to Adrienne. Tad ducked quietly behind the back of his car and made a wild dash back to the barn. In an instant Tad had Torque by the bridle, vaulted onto him and was flying through the yard towards the back of the farm.

"Mickey!" T.J. screamed frantically, "Mickey! He's got your horse!"

Jo Pilchard got out of her car and ran towards the young people as they all stood watching Tad disappear across the open fields on Torque.

"Well," she said, "this looks good. What the heck just went on over here? Are you O.K. Adrienne? I thought we *all* agreed not to confront that guy."

"Sorry Jo," Adrienne started to cry, "Tad was squashing the heck out of Phillip and I lost my cool. Oh, Mickey, I feel so bad, now he's gone and stolen your horse too!"

Mickey paused for a moment to think and took a deep breath. "It's just a horse Adrienne, I'm sure he'll be fine."

"I'm going after them," said T.J. running to the barn to get Dakotaroo.

"Not by yourself!" Mickey, Adrienne and Jo all said in unison.

Mickey took Adrienne by the shoulders and looked at her seriously, "I need your fastest horse. Torque's strong and he can work all day, but I'll need something with speed to catch him before Tad gets too far away."

"I'll go," said Adrienne, "Phillip, help me get Annie."

"Adrienne, I can't let you go, you're in no shape to ride and your mother would kill me if I let you," said Jo. "If it's Animation he needs, then let Mickey borrow your horse."

"Um, no, no, no, let's get something straight here, only Adrienne rides Adrienne's *nice* horse. I'm good at fast. I know the trails."

"We're wasting time," said Mickey agitated.

"Adrienne we need your horse now!" exclaimed T.J.

Phillip wailed "You feel bad that Mickey's horse got stolen, but not bad enough to lend him your horse! Adrienne, you're such a jerk! Tad's getting away."

"Fine," said Adrienne defeated, "but I need *you* to understand," she said to Mickey, "this horse, could possibly take me to the Olympics. I am allowed to do stupid things with her when my father is not around; *you,* are not."

"I'll take care of her, I promise," Mickey smiled, "and I'm only going because I know you can't, O.K."

"O.K." Adrienne said quietly.

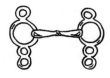

SIXTEEN

Dead Dog River

It was 7:47 p.m. when T.J. and Mickey set off on horseback to follow Torque. Jo, Adrienne and Phillip left in the police car to get to Bert Massey's barn quickly. They needed evidence fast. There had to be something, anything in the pile of stolen goods in the barn to link the crime to Tad. Constable Pilchard needed it now.

Mickey assumed that Tad would make a dash for the sugar shack to retrieve the treasure, his tracks; however, were leading the kids in pursuit far from Bert Massey's farm.

His trail was easy enough to follow. Torque's shoes had made deep footprints in the soft earth as he had galloped along.

"He's heading to the south," said T.J. as they kept their horses at a strong trot through a particularly rocky stretch of the forest far behind the Brooks' farm. "It doesn't make any sense."

"Why?" asked Mickey, "If he's trying to lose us why wouldn't he take us as far away from the Massey Farm as possible?"

"I don't know," said T.J. " It's just not right, it doesn't feel right, we never go this way with the horses, ever."

"Because?"

"Mickey, there are two places strictly forbidden to riders on horseback in this area, the Golf Course and the Dead Dog Scout Camp. Tad is taking us straight toward both. We never go this way. You get in big trouble for even setting foot in either of those two places, and there's a gorge and a river running right through the middle of the valley."

"Then it's easy," said Mickey, "he's going for the river. He's going to try and lose us there before he doubles back to get the treasure." He smiled and looked at Dakotaroo, "I *know* the Dakota horse can swim, will this mare go in the water?"

"Oh, yeah!" T.J. laughed, "Animation is like a crazy robot horse. She'll trust you and do *absolutely* anything you ask her to do. Did you ever want to jump a car?"

"Cool. No, but I'll try to remember she can if I need to later." Mickey halted Annie along the trail. The shadows were growing longer and the bush was thick with mosquitoes. The horses fussed. "Lets think about this for a minute," he said. "If we know that Tad is eventually going to make a run for Phillip's secret hiding place, then why don't we just ride there?"

"Because he's got your horse and it's more important to get Torque back in one piece than anything else."

"I suppose, and I'm a little bit afraid that if we lose him, he's just gonna take off with my horse and hold him hostage until he gets that stupid trunk. He has to think he's outsmarted us by losing us in the river before he'll think it's safe to go back to the sugar shack."

"Won't he be worried Jo and Phillip will get there first?"

"Oh, I'm sure he is, so he's going to want to lose us quickly. Mickey was quiet for a moment, he patted Annie on her neck, "Teej," he said looking off into the trees, "this is might sound kinda strange, but back home when we have to herd some cattle, we send out one fast rider to flank the whole herd while the other riders bring them along. Half the time, the dopey things don't even know the outrider is there, but they can't get away from the drive."

T.J. tilted her head to one side, "I don't think I understand."

"We know where Tad wants to go, and we need him to get there before us. I think we can fool him," he paused, "It means we're going to have to split up for a while. Right now he has no idea how many riders are chasing him. I'm going to leave and cut him off from the other side."

It was getting very dark. "Are you sure you can?" asked T.J.

"Pretty sure. I need you and Dakotaroo to keep chasing him, always be just where he expects you to be. If we're right and he's gonna make a run for Phillip's shack we'll never need to put our horses in the river. He hasn't seen us both yet, we have to do it now."

127

"O.K," T.J. tried not to sound nervous.

"Don't worry, I'll be closer than you think, I've done it a thousand times."

It was now cold enough that T.J. could see her breath. They were in unfamiliar country and she needed to be careful. The top edge of the ancient river valley was lined with a high limestone cliff. Giant pine trees loomed from the top, black against the stars. Dakotaroo picked her way slowly down the valley path toward the river, still following Tad's tracks. Mickey was nowhere to be seen. *Trust him*, thought T.J., the sound of the river was growing louder.

Animation's dark bay coat kept her well hidden in the forest. Every once in awhile a twig would snap loudly or a rock would roll down the hillside and crash into the river below. Mickey pushed her hard to canter downhill and reach the river before Tad. Finally, about 10 minutes after leaving T.J. behind, he found the water's edge and had Annie pick her way carefully along until he found a place where he could see the side of the river for quite a distance. There, in the shadows, he halted and asked Annie to wait.

The moon flashed off the surface of the water. If Mickey was correct, Tad would try to trick them by making a trail into the water, riding upstream for a little while and then leaving the river, on the same side as he came, to make his run for Bert's shack.

Suddenly Torque emerged from the trees and crashed his way into the cold, swirling river. The Dead Dog River was wide but not particularly deep. There were places where it ran fast and churned it's way through some giant rocks, but most of that was upstream. Torque splashed and scrambled through the rocks near the bank. Tad seemed to be trying to make as much noise as possible. Then he did something Mickey did not expect. Tad pushed Torque forward into the deeper water and crossed the river to the other side.

"Shoot," Mickey said to himself. He wanted badly to send Annie into the sparkling blackness of the river, but knew now he had to wait for T.J. so he could let her know Tad had gone all the way across. Luckily, T.J. was not far behind. Moments later Dakotaroo appeared where Tad had sent Torque into the river and stopped at the bank.

"He's gone across!" hollered Mickey to T.J. over the noise of the river. Water crashed around them. "I'm going to go follow him with Annie. You stay on this side of the river and meet Tad when he crosses back over upstream."

T.J. was getting cold, "Are you *sure* he's coming back this way?"

Mickey laughed, "T.J. if he's not, I'm gonna cut him off and keep crashing into him until he's back in the river. Trust me, he won't even know what hit him." At that, Annie plunged into the dark water and nimbly splashed her way through the rocks to the other side. "Keep moving upstream," he hollered back.

There was a narrow trail along the bank that had been made by hikers and anglers. Dakotaroo barely fit between the trees and the slippery sloping sides of the river, and needed to worm her way carefully along. T.J. took both feet out of her stirrups to raise her knees high and avoid being rubbed off by the trees. The river was increasingly deep and large boulders created dangerous rapids. T.J. traveled, for a long time along a stretch that no horse could ever swim across. It had become impossibly dark, so dark that she didn't see the bridge until they were mostly underneath it.

The Scout Camp Bridge. T.J. had been on it many times on foot, although no one was supposed to use it anymore. It was old and rickety, missing pieces of wood and held together with rope. Scary to cross on foot, it would be next to impossible to do on a horse, but suddenly Torque crashed through the trees on the other side, and made a run for it. Torque's coat glowed blue in the moonlight as he ran for the edge of the bridge and then stopped short just before crossing. Tad raised his whip and slashed him hard against his rump. The horse lurched forward and set foot on the bridge. It gently sagged under his weight. Torque flared his nostrils and made a long snorting noise. The next board he stepped on with a hind foot snapped in two and fell into the river below. Tad whipped him again, "Pay attention or that's you!" he hollered. Torque bolted for the other side of the bridge, jumping in great strides across the rotting lumber and scrambling as his legs scraped and crashed their way through. He was frothing and foaming from the mouth when they galloped past T.J. and Dakotaroo hidden in the trees. There were now giant holes in the rickety bridge. T.J. knew Mickey would never push Animation to cross it. Tad had bought himself some time by risking Torque's life to destroy the bridge. T.J. was beginning to feel sick.

Keep chasing him, always just where he expects you to be. Mickey's instructions rang in her head. T.J. leaned forward and whispered in the pony's ear. "C'mon Roo, let's get them."

It was easy to keep track of Tad and the horse as they climbed the long hill out of the valley. Tad was taking his time, seemingly unaware of T.J. right behind him. Torque glowed as if fluorescent. He had grown up on the Skyhouse farm in Montana, the rough terrain of hills and rocks was easy for him to climb. T.J. and Mickey had now been chasing them for over an hour. Silently Dakotaroo purred up the hill behind Torque. They were almost back to the top of the ridge when, in the valley below, T.J. heard Mickey and Annie splash back into the water far downstream.

Tad cocked his head to one side to listen. T.J. halted Dakotaroo in the dark and held her breath. *Luckily,* she thought, *most of Dakotaroo's white is on her back end.* Annie was silent again but it was too late. Tad raised his whip and sent Torque cantering hard up the last of the slope.

"If he hurts Torque I'll kill him!" T.J. said to Dakota aloud. "Well, maybe you could kill him. You can't go to jail." The footing was still rocky, slippery and wet. Neither horse could make very good time on top of the ridge and Tad had trouble going fast enough to get completely out of T.J.'s sight. Dakotaroo could have jumped many of the fallen logs on the old trail instead of going around them but T.J. did not want to risk hurting her. Soon they reached the flat, cultivated farmland at the edge of the valley and Torque and Tad hit their stride. Torque was fit and confident. Gleaming in the moonlight like a black and white ribbon through the fields they galloped ahead. Dakotaroo did her best not to lose any ground.

Tad crossed the Third Line without even slowing to check for traffic. He galloped straight across, Torque's hooves ringing on the pavement. T.J. slowed to look for cars, *it's night, there'd be headlights dummy, you'd see them for a long way off,* she tried to reassure herself, but still had to bring Dakotaroo back to a trot before she knew it was safe to cross the road. Seconds later, off to the south, Animation's hooves rang out on the pavement. T.J. smiled.

Torque did not tire. T.J. was getting tired. She adjusted her position in the saddle and lowered herself closer to Dakotaroo. "Come on Roo, please don't let them get away."

Tad veered to the left and galloped onto the rail trail. On the wide, bright path, there was no place for Dakotaroo to hide. Tad noticed them on his tail for the first time. *T.J.,* he thought smirking, *just T.J..* After weeks of stealing saddles in the dark, Tad was very familiar with the rail trail. He knew exactly how fast he could push Torque along and had a very good idea where the secret turn off to the sugar shack would be. T.J. was thankful for having him to follow, and was pretty sure she would not have found the path herself. Soon the footing had changed and the trees were spaced well apart. Dakotaroo knew the way.

Torque leaned hard into the first sharp turn and suddenly lost his footing.

Tad picked up his crop and whipped him hard on his haunches. "Get movin' you stupid mongrel."

The young horse jumped forward and flew off again even faster. Again and again Tad whipped him . Suddenly, while rounding the third corner since the beginning of the sugar bush trail, a dark horse flew in from the right, crashing it's way through the thick underbrush. The loud noise distracted Torque and in an instant caused him to quickly shy sideways and loose momentum. T.J. chased Dakota forward and caught up to Torque on the left.

"Catch him!" she hollered.

The three horses raced stride for stride through the dark blue forest. T.J. could taste salt and dirt and sweat all at the same time as she stayed down low in close to Dakota's mane. She turned her head quickly to the right to look at Torque.

Tad raised his whip again only this time, without warning, he brought it down hard against the haunches of Dakotaroo. The little horse showed the whites of her eyes and squealed as she leapt sideways. T.J. lost her left stirrup and was almost thrown off. Side by side Torque and Annie went flying down the trail. Dakotaroo was too small to keep up pursuit. It was a good thing. They had almost reached Phillip's secret shack. T.J. remembered the clothesline and bit her bottom lip, she had to stop them soon.

"Hold up!" she screamed, but the whistling wind just trapped the words from her mouth and blew them back behind her. "Hold up!"

There was only one way she could think of to make them stop the chase. She had to stop chasing. T.J. slowly pulled Dakotaroo to a halt. Mickey, looking back for her in the dark, suddenly noticed.

Torque slowed as Tad turned the curve and the sugar shack came into view. The big horse's nostrils flared and he let out a long snorting sound of protest. Torque remembered what lay up ahead. Annie dropped back to a trot. Torque slammed on the brakes hard about 300 meters from the corner of the shack.

Tad wholloped him hard on the haunches with his crop. " Get up there!" Torque pinned his ears back and danced on the spot.

He remembers. Thought T.J. glancing quickly from Torque to Mickey. "Hold up!" she yelled, this time loud enough to be heard.

"Say's who!" replied Tad angrily. "See if you ever find this precious horse again!" Tad turned and changing the grip on his crop, finally whipped Torque enough to send him flying forward again. 10

meters from the corner of the sugar shack Tad stood in his stirrups and waved goodbye.

T.J. winced as the plastic coated wire of Phillip's clothes line brushed over Torque's ears and caught Tad in the middle of his chest. With a loud cursing scream Tad Dillon came flying off the back of Torque and landed with a sickening thud in the middle of the sugar bush trail.

Before T.J. could speak, Dakotaroo flew off around the outside of the sugar shack and cantered quietly through the bush until she could catch up to the riderless Torque.

Animation halted only centimeters from stepping on Tad as he lay helplessly on the trail, groaning in a mess of leaves and mud. "What the heck do you think you're doing? I could have been killed by that stupid wire." Tad gasped for air and spit as he tried to sit himself upright. "Ahhhh! I think my leg is broken," he said weakly. His face was still red and swollen from where Adrienne had punched him, and two of his perfect teeth had been knocked out by his fall.

"I don't want to help him." T.J. said looking away and trying hard not to cry.

"Hey, slow down, don't worry," said Mickey looking up at her on Dakotaroo and rubbing the little mare's face kindly. "Torque's safe now, and Tad's not going anywhere," he smiled, "You did a good job Teej."

Looking down at Tad, helpless and stuck in the mud, the thing T.J.

still most wanted to do in the whole world, was walk over and kick him.

Tad tried to move away again. He had broken his left femur just above the knee, and his leg was bent behind at a horrible, twisted angle. He screamed as he tried to move, and then decided it was best that he just remain very, very still.

"O.K., this guy may be a jerk, but that still doesn't mean we can leave him here in the bush all by himself. We can't move him and who knows how long it will be before help arrives."

"Jo and Phillip will be on their way," T.J. said shivering. She dismounted Dakotaroo and thought quietly for a moment. "Adrienne's brother uses this old shack as a clubhouse for him and his goat. I know for sure that he has blankets and food and stuff in there. There are probably matches in there too so we can build a fire until they find us."

Tad groaned.

"Tad might go into shock, he could use a blanket," said Mickey. "Do you want to wait here T.J. or would you rather go search the shack?"

T.J.'s eyes were well adjusted to the dark. "I don't really believe he's hurt," she said quietly. "I mean, what if he's faking it and one of us leaves. What if I go and he jumps up and grabs you?"

"He won't, he'd never catch me. Anyhow, if you take a good look at his face you can tell he isn't faking anything. He's hurtin' bad T.J. I think it's safe to leave him for a while, he's not goin' anywhere."

SEVENTEEN

Aliens Alone

Phillip's sugar shack was *very* creepy in the dark. T.J. cautiously pushed open the old wooden plank door. She shone the flashlight briefly around the room, and suddenly, something inside crashed down to the floor. T.J. screamed, quickly shut the door again and pushed her back up against it.

Mickey put his hand on the door beside her ear and gave it a push. "T.J." he mocked, "who would be out here in the cold in this crappy old shack?"

"Aliens? Phillip talks a lot about aliens," she replied meekly, turning the flashlight again to survey the room. The reflection of two bright green eyes glowed back at her. T.J. gasped.

"Relax, It's just a big ol' raccoon, see." He held her by the shoulders and made her face the raccoon. "Besides, aliens never want to be *this* cold," he smiled mischievously, "*aliens* prefer the desert."

"Shoo!" she tried to frightened the fat thief out the front door. It ambled fearlessly past her and out without a complaint.

Mickey quietly explored the shack while T.J. set about gathering up anything she felt they may need for the night. She grabbed a pillow, a blanket, an unopened bag of tortilla chips, eight cans of pop, some chocolate left over from Easter, a book of matches, and a magazine about video games to use to start the fire. T.J. hoped Phillip would not miss the magazine much. He only had about a hundred video game magazines to choose from.

"What *is* this?" asked Mickey confused. On a long shelf, along one wall of the shack, over thirty glass jars of light amber liquid had been meticulously set in a line. Each jar had been carefully labeled with Phillip's name and a date.

"Oh, Phillip collects his pee." T.J. joked.

"Really?" Mickey squinted to look at the jars more closely. "Why would he put the date on it?"

"No!" admitted T.J. laughing. "It's maple syrup. Phillip spent all spring making it here. That's what a sugar shack is for, you boil down the sap from the maple trees here, in the bush. Phillip's a weird kid but not really 'saving his pee in jars' kind of weird."

"Good thing."

T.J. put the matches carefully in her pocket and gathered everything else up in the blanket like a sack.

"What is Tad short for, Theodore or something?" Mickey asked as they walked back to where Tad lay in a heap under the tree.

"I don't know? Maybe Tadwell or Tadrick, Adrienne likes to call him Tad-pole."

"Edward," groaned Tad, "It's Edward you losers."

"Easy there buddie, do you want some first aid with that leg there or what?" Mickey asked kindly. "I've got some supplies, we can bind it to your other leg but you'll have to co-operate."

"Leave me alone." Tad hissed, grabbing the blanket Mickey held out to him.

"Do you have the time T.J.?" Mickey squinted at her and tapped his watch, "I don't even know what time zone we're in here." His gold Mickey Mouse watch read 10:06 p.m.

"Eastern," said T.J., pushing the sleeve of her shirt up until she could read her watch. "Um, it's just after midnight, 12:06 a.m."

"So two hours ahead," he said. "I keep forgetting."

T.J. smiled, "You *could* just change the time on your watch, eh.?"

Mickey looked slightly embarrassed. "Then I wouldn't know what time it was at home, now would I. I like to know what time it is at home."

It was then that T.J. remembered Mickey's uncle Dennison had once told her how homesick he had been while away studying in England. "Hey," she said, "how was Europe?"

"It was O.K., saw a lot of old stuff."

"Just O.K.? I think it would be *so* cool to spend a whole month

139

traveling through old castles and ruins and things. It was just O.K.?"

Mickey had started a fire and poked the first tiny glowing embers with a long stick. "I…I don't really like to travel alone. I don't know, maybe it was just a bad idea. My parents died in a plane crash, did I ever tell you that? They had a really cool plane we used to trip all over the place with. Spending 6 hours crossing the Atlantic Ocean only gave me a lot of time to think about how much I missed them."

T.J. was quiet for a moment trying to think of the right thing to say. "You know next time I'd be more than happy to go with you." She smiled, passing him a big piece of Phillip's leftover Easter chocolate, "Adrienne too, Adrienne's always up for a crazy trip."

"Thanks," he said, "next time you're invited."

"So, you're still planning to leave Palouse River to go to High School in Connecticut this Fall, or is that going to be a bad idea too?" she asked.

"Um, yes, but that's kinda why I'm here. Well, that and the whole lonely-in-Europe thing. I've talked Uncle Den into letting me take Torque to Connecticut with me in September."

"No way! That's awesome!" said T.J.

"Yeah, I really had to beg, and promise to keep my grades up. That means he'll need to stay here a little longer though. I was going to take him home at the end of July but there's really no point in hauling Torque all the way to Montana just to turn around and come back again.

Would you keep him a bit longer for me?"

T.J. blushed, and was glad that it was too dark for Mickey to see. "Mickey, Torque was just stolen, he could have been killed. Do you really want us to keep him for you longer."

"Hey that was my fault! I was too dumb to hang on to him when there was a crazy guy around. I'm from a pretty crazy town, I should know better!"

The horses suddenly became restless.

"Someone is coming up the trail," whispered T.J. startled.

Flashlight beams bounced along the ground and off the trees. A jolly loud voice came out of the dark.

"Phillip!" T.J. cheered.

Together Phillip, Adrienne, Arleen and Jo Pilchard walked out of the dark and into the firelight. Constable Pilchard had brought another young officer for assistance.

"Hey, this looks rather cozy," exclaimed Phillip. He was carrying Tad's "Adrienne" wig in his right hand.

"Oh, I'm so relieved we've found you guys at last." Arleen ran over to embrace T.J.

"Mr. Dillon." Jo Pilchard's partner loomed large over Tad. "We would like you to come with us. You have a lot of explaining to do son."

Tad sat quietly looking at the ground. If he could have, he would have run off into the bush. They had him. T.J. and Mickey had tracked him down and turned him in. Phillip Brooks would pay for this.

"Get up!" The officer pulled Tad by the collar of his coat.

"Aaahhhh." Tad howled in pain. "I'm hurt you stupid jerk! Do you think I'd be just sittin' around the campfire with *these* two if I didn't have to?"

Mickey walked over to where Tad sat on the ground. Tad's left foot pointed in completely the wrong direction. It looked really disturbing. "He broke his leg when he fell off the horse. He needs first aid but refused to let us help him." Mickey pointed to Tad's leg with his right hand as he talked, and seven large gold rings came alive in the firelight.

The policeman's eyes grew wide as he quickly calculated the immense value of the gold on Mickey's hand. "That's a lot of jewelry you've got there son. Hope you can prove ownership of all that hardware. Maybe this kid had better come along with us too Jo," he said.

T.J. froze, she had never heard anyone question Mickey about his gold.

"My father," he began, looking up and capturing the detective with his stare. "My father was the leading aboriginal defense attorney in the United States. He died about two years ago when he crashed his twin engine Piper Seminole into Mount Hewlett in northern Oregon.

The rings were his."

Jo Pilchard took the young officer by the arm,. "It's O.K. Brad, the kid's cool, the rings are his. It's early morning and I'm sure we're all quite tired." Jo smiled warmly at Mickey and winked. "We'll take Mr. Dillon here back with us and, if it's O.K. with you Mrs. Brooks, we'll leave you to sort out what to do with the rest of these young people."

Phillip had put Tad's "Adrienne" wig on while no one was paying attention to him.

Adrienne rolled her eyes at him but decided not to make a fuss. It was funny, and although it had taken her years to figure out, Adrienne knew that the best way to handle Phillip's most annoying behavior was to ignore him.

"That's fine," said Arleen brushing her hair back from her eyes.

"Hey," said Phillip still in the wig, "Tad has my key!"

"Yeah," said Adrienne, "give the poor little kid back his key you jerk."

Jo looked seriously at Tad, "Mr. Dillon, I believe you have Phillip's key."

"I don't know what they're talking about," Tad replied coldly.

Jo reached for her handcuffs, "Mr. Dillon, you are in a lot of trouble, you are also badly hurt and will need our help to ever leave this forest. If I were you, I'd give the little kid back his key."

"Hey!" objected Phillip, "you can all drop the 'little kid' thing thanks."

Tad slowly handed over the skeleton key and sneered at the girls as the police set his leg. Jo radioed for an O.P.P four wheeler to meet them on the rail trail and transport Tad out of the forest.

"I'll be in touch in the morning." said Jo as they walked slowly away carrying Tad Dillon in a stretcher made from the blanket.

EIGHTEEN

Bert Massey

Mickey brought a fresh armload of wood and put it on the fire. "May I offer you something to drink Mrs. Brooks?" he asked, "We have a fine selection of orange soda."

"No, thank you." she smiled politely and then was quiet for a moment. "Laura Petty has disappeared. Constable Jo told us so on the way over." said Arleen. "Did you guys know that she was Mr. Massey's step daughter?"

"Really!" said Adrienne, "Get out! The old dude was married once!"

Mickey sat silently down beside T.J. to listen and quietly opened a can of pop. "Hang on," he sighed, "go back, who *are* these people? The new kid is having a hard time keepin' up."

"Sorry," said Mrs. Brooks, reaching for a handful of chips. "Let me tell you what I know."

"Bert Massey grew up on the farm on the fourth line," she began. "As a young man he traveled the world, and I'm fairly certain he fought for Canada in the second world war. When his parents were elderly, they convinced him to come home and run the farm. He raised prize winning Southdown sheep and also bred horses. As a young girl I remember him letting us come to see the new lambs. There were always lots and lots of lambs. Bert's mother lived to be very old. He cared for her, drove her to church and things like that, but never seemed to find a wife of his own. The year his mother died, he met Emily Petty late one night on the fourth line when her car got stuck in the snow and he pulled her out with his tractor. Emily was widowed at the time, and had one daughter from her first marriage, Laura." Arleen stopped and yawned, "Do you really want to hear all this?"

"Yes, of course!" said T.J.

"Bert was also the first person I ever knew to own an Appaloosa," Arleen continued. "You hardly ever saw them when I was a kid, just in circuses and stuff." She took a handful of chips, and in the dark by the firelight, T.J. noticed for the first time how much Arleen really was like Adrienne. "He had a mare that he used to show all over North America after his mom passed away, just before he met Emily Petty. It's funny, I remember that mare as really tall and very beautiful, but she was probably actually pretty short and looked like an Appaloosa!" Arleen

146

laughed.

"Easy there!" protested Mickey.

"So whatever happened to the horse?" asked T.J. wide eyed.

"I don't remember exactly how or why it happened, but everyone knew that when he asked Emily Petty to marry him, Laura was very upset. To try and win her over, Bert gave his new stepdaughter the beautiful horse as a gift. She never wanted it, or cared for it. The mare lived on Bert's farm, out with the sheep for years, until about 15 years ago when Emily Petty died. Bert came home one afternoon and she was gone."

"Gone?" said Adrienne.

"Gone! Laura had sold her and moved her away while he was out."

"That's awful," said T.J., "did he ever get her back?"

"No," Arleen shook her head, "he was in his seventies, his wife had just died and the horse was very old. Soon his sheep were all gone too. Laura convinced everyone that he was too feeble to take care of them and she moved them all away."

"That's so bad. Didn't he ever fight her for them," asked Phillip

"He tried, but I think he was afraid. Afraid that if she could take his animals, then really none of his treasures were safe."

"So he stayed at home?"

"Yep," replied Arleen.

"Always?" asked Mickey.

"Almost always, he went to the fair every year, I think," added Phillip. "I met him there once."

"So Bert and Laura were at war for years?" Adrienne asked.

"Sometimes families are like that," Mickey answered, "Sometimes people even forget what made them so angry in the first place, but they just can't stop. They've gone too far. Dug a hole too deep."

"Bert knew why he was angry, she sold his horse!" said T.J.

"Yeah, I guess it all came to a head when Dakotaroo went missing."

"Tad said Laura told Bert she'd help him find Dakotaroo, if he gave her the Lion." Phillip said quietly, he had now pulled the long hair of the Adrienne wig into a single pony tail like Mickey's.

"What lion?" they asked in unison.

Phillip held up the silver key in the firelight. "I guess in the morning we'll see."

NINETEEN

Dakotaroo

"It's under here," he said. "I remembered seeing this in a movie once. You move the table, roll back the carpet and then have to dig a hole in the floor. I already had it hidden this way when T.J. suggested I bury the trunk. I'm pretty sure it would have slowed down Tad a bit." He smiled as he unveiled the carpet and began digging in the floor. The trunk was not very deep.

Clunk, the camp shovel hit the green metal hard. Phillip, Mickey, T.J. and Arleen together lifted it from its grave.

"Gee Phillip, what the heck is in here? Rocks?" asked Mickey sarcastically.

"Maybe," Phillip said with a smile. The morning sun filtered through the old glass windows and played a pattern on the trunk as it sat on the floor. Phillip pulled the slender silver key out of his pocket and looked at it closely.

"Cross your fingers," he whispered, "here goes nothin'" The key turned smoothly in the lock. Phillip smiled as it clicked ever so softly.

Slowly he lifted the latch and opened the lid.

T.J. gasped.

On top of a large pile of square granite rocks was a thick well worn notebook. Large Black letters had been carefully drawn across it's cover. "For Theresa Jane Thompson."

Adrienne lifted the scrapbook from the chest and turned the first page. It was a book about Dakotaroo. There were pictures of her as a foal, pictures of T.J. that Bert Massey had taken at the Fall Fair, newspaper articles about her disappearance. Bert had kept them all. She had been as special to him as a foal as she was to T.J. now. On the last page of the scrapbook was a short handwritten note.

> Dear Theresa,
> Thank you for taking such wonderful care of
> Dakota. I have enjoyed watching you for many years.
> Together you remind me of the happiest days of my whole life,
> and I know that you love her just as much as I loved her
> mother. Please take The Lion of Shalasa to help you find her,
> and use it's value to help you keep her always.
> Your friend, Albert James Massey.

"That's kinda creepy Teej." said Adrienne looking over her shoulder. She read it again aloud.

"So Bert's horse was Dakotaroo's mom?" Phillip asked.

T.J. shuddered. "What is a Lion of Sha-la-sa?" she said slowly.

Under the scrapbook lay a small box. Phillip lifted it from within the rocks and opened the lid.

"The Lion of Shalasa," he presented her with the box cupped in two hands, "It's the largest diamond ever found in Ethiopia. Bert found it over 50 years ago when he was working in Africa." he explained. "It's worth about a million bucks. Laura Petty knew he had it in the trunk and that he had decided to give it to you. He told her he was going to. That's why they had a big fight right before he died. Laura didn't want him to give you the jewel, he knew you needed the money to find Dakotaroo."

"But why would he fill the trunk with rocks?"

"So it wouldn't be easy to steal. Trust me, it took every ounce of strength Tad and I had just to move the darn thing out of the house and into the barnyard. It'd be pretty hard for two guys to lift it onto a truck."

"How'd y'all get it here by yourself?" Mickey asked.

"Pez dragged it through the bush."

"So *you* had the trunk, and Robbie had the key."

T.J. looked at the diamond and touched it softly. It was as large as a robin's egg and surrounded in white velvet. When Dakotaroo was missing, when T.J. was so sad and only she, Adrienne and Phillip had believed they would ever find her beautiful horse again; Bert Massey was ready to give T.J. his most prized possession to help get Dakotaroo back. She wanted to cry.

"What a cool old guy," said Adrienne.

"Yeah, I think so. I've read a lot about his adventures lately," said Phillip going up on the tips of his toes and pulling down a shoebox from one of the shelves. "Here, I bought this box of photos when they auctioned off all his stuff. I like this one of him at the pyramids, and this one, look it's Cowboy Bert." Cowboy Bert, about 50, was standing in a show ring of young Appaloosa horses. A beautiful young girl was presenting Bert and his horse with a large silver plate. He wore a big white cowboy hat and was grinning from ear to ear. The banner behind them read Montana State Fair, in the distance you could see mountains.

T.J. could almost hear the coyotes.

Shocked by the photo, Mickey quietly picked it up and looked at both sides carefully, again and again. T.J. was watching him and smiled sheepishly when Mickey's eyes met hers, she could tell he knew the young woman well.

"Phillip, may I have this photo?" Mickey asked.

"Sure, if you like it, take it."

Mickey removed his wallet from his hip pocket. The first of the morning sun danced in the gold on his fingers. He carefully pulled out the well worn photo of his favourite horse Skyblue and quietly put the picture of his mother and Bert Massey beside it.

About the Author

Krista Michelle Breen lives in Rockwood, Ontario, with her 2 children, Walker and Aniela and her husband Doug. Krista's grade school teachers repeatedly asked her to stop talking about horses, stop writing about horses and to please draw something other than horses. She Graduated from the University of Guelph in 1990 with a Bachelors of Science in Agriculture. After graduation Krista spent eight years working for The City of Toronto at Riverdale Farm and today spends her time coaching and training young horses and riders in Hillsburgh Ontario. She is an Equine Canada certified Instructor and Canadian Pony Club Alumni. Hardware is her second novel.